AMELIA O'DONOHUE IS SO NOT A VIRGIN

HELEN FITZGERALD

sourcebooks
fire

Cover and internal design © 2010 by Sourcebooks, Inc.
Cover design by JenniferJackman.com
Cover images © Con Tanasiuk/Design Pics/Corbis, Kenneth O'Quinn/iStock photo

Sourcebooks and the colophon are registered trademarks of Sourcebooks, Inc.

Published by Sourcebooks Fire, an imprint of Sourcebooks, Inc.
P.O. Box 4410, Naperville, Illinois 60567-4410
(630) 961-3900
Fax: (630) 961-2168
teenfire.sourcebooks.com

Library of Congress Cataloging-in-Publication data is on file with the publisher.

Printed and bound in the United States of America.
VP 10 9 8 7 6 5 4 3 2 1

For my wonderful, funny daughter, Anna Casci

CHAPTER ONE

I t was a typical breakfast except for two things.

The typical things:

1. My mother sighed heavily and stared into space.
2. Dad found corrupt politicians in *The Scotsman* and it made his lips go green.

Not typical things:

1. The doorbell rang. It was Matt the postman with my fourth year exam results, as well as a congratulatory letter from the head teacher.
2. I screamed.

History: A (top of class)

Physics: A (top of class)

Math: A (top of class)

English: A (equal top with Louisa MacDonald, who rang later hoping she'd beaten me but she hadn't. Ha!)

Chemistry: A (top of class)

Biology: A (top of the world)

I blurted out my results to my mother and my father.

Just so you know, it had been a long time since I'd thought of my mother and my father as *Mum* and *Dad*. Mum and Dad, in my opinion, indicated some kind of intimacy, and I didn't have any with my mother and my father. Not because of some massive disaster—like my mother drinking, or like my father bashing her head in with a saucepan when dinner's crap, or like the death of a younger, better sibling—but because my mother and my father were emotional retards.

When I told my mother my results, she said, "Hard work pays off." She had finished staring into space.

My father said, "Don't let it go to your head." He had finished with *The Scotsman*.

But it was too late. It had *so* gone to my head that I screamed then rang all my friends.

And they were like, "Really?"

"I know; I can't believe it!"

My ruddy-cheeked pal, Katie Bain, said, "We should cele-brate! I've got it! A brisk walk to the standing stones and a picnic of Mum's homemade oatcakes and Mrs. Goslan's famous black-berry jam! Oh, and a thermos of hot chocolate! Steaming!"

Katie Bain only ever spoke with exclamation marks. I said maybe another time. There was a call waiting.

It was Louisa. She seemed a bit pissed off.

"But you did really well too!" I said.

(But not as well as me!)

Straight As.

Top of the class.

Top of the school in fact.

And my enormous success stayed in my head right up till dinner, by which time I'd ridden my bike all the way down my drive, along the two-mile coastal road and into the village to show the piece of paper to all of the above and their parents and their brothers and their sisters.

Only Louisa seemed interested in my results.

Her folks owned Aulay's whitewashed pub. Aulay's and the church bookended the seaside strip of fifteen houses and three shops. In her cozy bedroom above the bar, she read the letter with a scrunched up face, checking to see if they'd made a mistake, then said, *Wow!* The others said, *Oh great, gotta go to the post office/Pick some rosemary/You really should come to the standing stones!*

So when I got home for supper, a fog of anticlimax had settled over me. Who cared if I did well? What would it change anyways?

As if to prove my theory, my mother told me to go to bed

at the stupidly early hour of 9:00 p.m. and said, "Say your prayers. Ask for humility."

"Please god can I have some humility," I said out loud.

She was like, "Properly."

"Please god *may* I have some humility," I said.

"And ask for forgiveness."

"Please god forgive me…" I obeyed, then opened my eyes a tad and looked at my mother, who was standing over me, steely faced…"What for?"

"For your sins."

"For my sins and god bless my mother and god bless my father and please may I go to Aberfeldy Halls. Amen."

I wanted to go to Aberfeldy Halls more than anything in the entire universe. Louisa MacDonald and Mandy Grogan were going there. It was the best senior boarding school in the highlands. It had the best science grades in the UK. Nine out of ten graduates went on to university after going there.

I needed to go to university. I needed to do medicine and make money and live in the city, maybe even in London. At Aberfeldy Halls, you got your own cubicle and you studied for four hours every night. You got two choices for dinner. You got big shiny science labs and literature teachers who came from exotic countries and also wrote novels.

The outcome of my wish depended on the good lord apparently. (I am deliberately not using capitals.)

My mother said, "The good lord will tell us if you should go to Aberfeldy Halls. If you listen hard enough, you will hear."

Listening to the good lord was very dull. Especially on Sundays, when the whole island did nothing but listen to the good lord, their ears pricked as they sat still in their living room seats, bibles in hand. No ferries; no cars; no shops; no television, talking, music, nothing. Just listening, waiting to be saved. From what? From boredom? From hour-like-minutes that ticked a sharp bird-beak into your skull?

They had plans for me, my parents. They wanted me, their only child, to stay on the island and be safe: tucked away from the evils and temptations of the city. They wanted me in our small croft house, where the ghosts of wet farmers from two hundred years ago lived with the ghosts of us. They wanted me to go to the local state school—a gray seventies scar on the outskirts of the village—where teachers yawned and pupils' shoulders lowered with the hours. They wanted me to get just enough education to handcuff me to some god-fearing McFarmer for the rest of my life.

I had different plans. I longed to leave the island, my floating prison of rain, hunched shoulders, and the good lord. I was no

Katie Bain. I didn't have red hair, freckles, and a cheeky grin. I didn't collect rocks on beaches and get into mischief on hillocks. I didn't want to know everyone or everything about them. I'd only lived in the city till I was nine, but I knew I was a city girl. I'd loved Edinburgh. I'd loved our old flat, a top floor tenement the size of Dundee, with floor-to-ceiling windows that looked out over the floodlit Castle, with neighbors who minded their own business, and with hide-and-seek nooks and crannies like the old maid's room above the kitchen. When I used to open the bedroom window in my childhood flat, noises would fly at me: buses honking, people talking, even bagpipes piping from the touristy Princes Street. When I used to step outside, I'd be confronted with at least ten different things to do: Milkshake here? Dinner there? Movies over the road? Theatre round the corner? Dungeon up the hill? When I stepped out of the croft house, on the other hand, I was only ever confronted with a wind that bit my tonsils off.

I wanted crowds, noise, anonymity, difference. And I figured if I got a really good education, my parents couldn't argue.

They'd say, "You got into Oxford?"

And I'd say, "I did!"

And they'd be like, "Well done, Rachel! You were right to go to Aberfeldy Halls. We're proud of you."

Because while my parents were emotional retards, I wanted to make them proud. I wanted to make them see that to be saved you must first dive into the water. If I dove first, perhaps they would follow. Perhaps they would be happy again.

• • •

The next morning, I decided that I needed to take serious action if my plan was ever going to work. I made my mind up that I would lie to my mother and my father. We were eating salty porridge at the kitchen table.

"I heard him," I said.

"What was that?" my father asked, not looking up from the corrupt politicians in *The Scotsman*.

"The good lord spoke. He told me I would go," I said.

They'd never explained to me exactly how the good lord might tell us stuff, so I had no idea if this would work.

My mother squinted, staring at me, wondering.

"Last night. Clear as day…'*Rachel, you are going to Aberfeldy Halls.*'" (I said this in a very deep godlike voice.)

"In that voice?"

"*his* voice. No doubt about it. I had been listening very hard."

My mother was like, "Stop your nonsense."

My father said, "That's blasphemy, Rachel. Go to your room."

I vowed there and then that when I visited them in their

ocean-view island retirement home and they turned to me and whispered, "I've been saved." I would say, "Stop your nonsense and go to hell!"

My parents' punishments had always been clear, firm, and followed-through-to-the-letter. When I was nine, they grounded me for seven days solid after I'd dropped my crisps in the back of the car and said the f word. When I was eleven, they grounded me for two weeks (no telephone calls or television) because I'd kissed a boy called James Connor in a game of Truth or Dare at Louisa MacDonald's birthday party (Louisa's older sister told her aunt, etc., etc.).

So when they asked me to go to my room, I obeyed, because not obeying would have serious repercussions. I spent hours lying on my bed dreaming of cinemas with movies from France and Germany, of Vietnamese restaurants, of people wearing strange hats and/or huge sunglasses, of markets selling crazy big bubble machines and vintage coats in all shapes and sizes.

Please, please oh non-existent god, I said out loud, *may I go to Aberfeldy Halls.*

CHAPTER TWO

It was a whopping 72 degrees the next day.

"Nah, I don't want to go for a swim," I said when John got Mandy Grogan to ring and ask if I'd meet him at the beach at 12:00. Truth was, my period had arrived, and I hadn't made the transition from pads to tampons. I'd tried a few times, lying on the floor of the bathroom, eyes closed (too hard), squeezing at a space that simply did not exist.

"Anyways, I need to work on my mother," I told Mandy.

So instead of swimming, which would have meant harboring a monstrous cotton surfboard in the pants of my swimsuit which in turn would have swelled and disintegrated in the water, I spent the morning fencing. This did not involve cool silver outfits and a long weapon, but kneeling in the mud hammering nails into the wooden poles that kept our sheep in their waterlogged paddocks. Mum bought the sheep for her "hobby farm," a euphemism for the fact that she was unemployed and bored out of her mind since moving north.

Our farm consisted of two large paddocks that swept down from our ancient white house to the ocean. People from London would probably pay thousands of pounds to come here for Hogmanay—which is how we celebrate New Year's Eve here—and marvel at our thatched roof and light our wood fire and walk over our paddocks. They'd call it beautiful and quaint and full of history and mystery. I call it shitesville.

By the time I came in for lunch (roast lamb on white bread—the poor buggers always ended up in my sandwiches), I was wheezing.

"You're wheezing," Mum said.

"No I'm not."

"You need to go to bed for a while."

"No I don't. I'm fine."

In my room, I read the leaflet in my tampon packet again, unwrapped one of the offending items, and said to myself, *Right, this is stupid. You can do anything you set your mind to. You can do this. Even Mandy can do this, and she got D for History.*

I wobbled my head from side to side and breathed out (two three) then placed one leg on a chair and breathed out (two three) again, and then, realizing no amount of breathing out (two three) and body wobbling would actually relax me, I placed the white object in the general direction (I hoped) of its target, closed my eyes, scrunched my face, and pushed with all my might. I sometimes watched those television shows about surgery—scalpels cutting and gloved hands going places they best not—and this felt the same to me. I had entered a space that was blood and gutsy. I retrieved my tamponless finger and perched myself on the edge of my bed. The thing had only gone in half way, perhaps due to my eye-scrunching-body-tension. And when I finally gathered the courage to stand up I felt like I'd pushed Mandy's horse Dusty inside me. It was so obviously *there*, like someone had shoved a conker up my nostril. But there was a space, which was a relief, because if there hadn't been one, I'd have been a properly weird female. So I tried to ignore it, moving one leg around the other towards my bedroom door and out.

I waddled down our driveway, across the road, and onto the beach. There are tourist pictures of the beaches on our island. Smiling women in bikinis lie in uncomfortably flattering poses on soft white sand, basking in the sun, spectacular mountains behind, a bright blue sea before, beckoning you to swim in me, swim in me, now. Truth is, Scottish beaches are like polar bears—they both look nice in photographs. Pat a polar bear, it'll kill you. Stand on a Scottish beach, you'll realize how shit it is. There's only one beach on the island that looks a bit like the one in the brochures, and I have never seen anyone swim in it. It's freezing. And the water is kind of gray, like the sky is most of the time. And the wind is always howling. And that's only one beach. The rest of them are like the one across the road from my farm, which is a perfect teenage meeting place in that it is the kind of beach that no adult in their right mind would want to go to. Most of Ross beach (I named it that) is black and rocky. Mossy grass stops where the volcanic gunge starts, and this ends with water that is not only freezing but laden with jaggy rocks that make a paddling experience one of pain and inevitable scabs.

Just ignore it, ignore it, I said, as I shuffled along the black rocky strip. *There is no conker inside me. Breathe.* I could spot Mandy's bikini a mile away. It was bright red with yellow dots, one of the numbers Mandy got on her biannual shopping spree in Glasgow.

Mandy had been my best friend since I'd arrived. We had nothing in common; Mandy believed in god, loved the island, hated schoolwork, and wanted to be a hairdresser—but she was a very relaxing, uncomplicated person to be around. She was short and cute, with curly blonde hair and a constant smile, and was the most fashionable girl within miles. We never fought, despite spending an incredible amount of time together, riding our bikes, riding her horse, drinking tea like old ladies, giggling, and reading (her: magazines; me: textbooks). I loved her.

As I got closer to Mandy, I noticed her red with yellow dots were entwined with some blue board shorts. In the latter was Mandy's boyfriend, Andrew: an incomer with a huge house on the south of the island. Being the new boy in town, all the girls had their eyes on him, but Mandy nabbed him with her nearly-C cups and her willingness. About a week after they got together, Mandy started wearing jumpers with huge floppy turtlenecks.

"Nice jumper," I'd lied. It wasn't very nice at all.

"It's my concealer," she'd said, taking me into her bedroom and lowering the neck. Underneath was an almighty love-bite. Looked like he'd sucked so hard her subclavian artery had erupted.

It had faded a bit since then, but clad only in bikinis, stripped bare of her turtleneck concealer, her neck still looked damaged. She and Andrew were snogging furiously, half-sitting, half-lying on a big green towel.

John was lying face down on a towel beside them.

"So are you ready yet?" he asked, sitting up.

John was the same age as me—sixteen. He was five-ten, with shoulder length blonde hair, unusually tanned skin, sparkly blue eyes, long dark eyelashes, and crooked teeth. We'd met at school. His family was full of media types who worked from home and traveled a lot, and he was going to be an actor. Like all the boys in our school, he wanted to go out with Mandy, but she was already with Andrew, and I didn't mind being second choice when he'd expressed interest at the village dance. Boys weren't high on my agenda. In fact, I thought John would be better off with someone sillier and taller, like Grace (the butcher's daughter), who never said the wrong thing to boys and was apparently gagging for it. But if he wanted me, then what the hell?

Our first snog was *so* not romantic. The power in the village hall had gone down due to high winds. Mandy's candle flickered my way and she told me John asked her to ask me if I wanted to go out with him…and I told her to say yes and he asked her to ask me if I would do a bit more than just snog him and I asked her to tell him I didn't know if I was ready to do that yet…but he told her to tell me yes anyway and then he came over to me and this is what he said:

"Like they say in the films"—he pronounced it *fillems*—"this is very romantic." And I winced 'cause it was a terrible, nausea-inducing line, but I snogged him anyways in the corner of the hall, and his tongue was so dry it shredded bits of mine off—and before I knew it, he was sucking on my neck as if a serial killer was chasing his car and he'd run out of petrol north of Ullapool (or somewhere equally godforsaken), and he'd come across an abandoned truck with a full, unlocked tank of it, and for the life of him he had to suck the petrol out or he'd die, DIE. And then he stopped sucking just in time to save my internal organs from combusting, not-spontaneously, and I know I made that word up, but I made it up 'cause it's totally what I would have done if he hadn't stopped, which is what he did when the lights came back on.

And that was that. We were a couple. And for a month, he'd meet me at the beach and say, "So, are you ready yet?" and I'd say no, and he'd insert his huge sandpaper tongue into my mouth then suck my neck like there was no tomorrow, and then try to do more anyways and I'd say, "No!" Which is exactly what I said this time, taking off my shorts and T-shirt and doing the unthinkable and running uncomfortably into the icy water.

Oh dear, something was happening down there. The thing was expanding, probably because it wasn't all in. I could feel it filling with water and growing.

"When will you know?" John asked, having followed me into the ocean.

We were both shivering. The water had stolen the nerve endings in our lower bodies.

But I could feel something. The *thing*. It was getting larger and larger. I wondered, would it expand until I exploded, or would my legs end up in the splits-position, an enormous mountain of wet red cotton my inflatable raft?

I couldn't speak. I wanted him to go away before the climax of this terrible tampon tragedy.

"Are you all right?"

"Yes," I said. But no, I wasn't. It was gigantic and fleeing. Unplugging. Only in about a millimeter, I reckoned.

"It can only lead to one thing," I explained, trying to press my legs together.

I'd been aware I wasn't ready for sex for some time. The idea made me feel terrified. Like letting someone read my diary or watch me on the toilet. It conjured the same feelings as bungee jumping and touching huge hairy spiders. If the tampon was anything to go by, I was right to be scared.

"Well then you're chucked," John said, turning and walking out of the water.

"What?"

"You're chucked!" He grabbed his towel and walked away.

Mandy was still snogging Andrew. I could see her tongue

going into his cheek and pushing it like he was saying "Dah!"

I was chucked. I had a stray rat-size-plug in my bikini bottoms.

And the skies were opening and cracking and banging and letting loose the wrong amount of rain.

• • •

My mother said, "Where have you been?"

"Just hanging around with Mandy," I said through juddering teeth.

"You don't look well," my mother said.

"I'm fine."

I wasn't. The perfect recipe for my usual flu-asthma fanfare. Warm weather followed by torrential rain and an immediate drop in temperature of ten degrees.

Since I was nine, I'd had an asthma attack approximately once a year. Always in summer. Always resulting in hospitalization, which I hated, hated, hated.

I raced to the bathroom to unleash my enormous tailed rat, went to bed with a pad, a definite wheeze, a bit of a sore tummy, and a bit of a headache. Within an hour I had a raging headache, a raging temperature, and a raging sore tummy. Two hours later, I couldn't breathe at all. Perched on the edge of my bed, I made breathing-like noises, but no air was going in and my face was bright red and I couldn't even yell for my mother, who did not like to have her private times interrupted, who did not like daughters creeping in and maybe seeing something she shouldn't—like that time when I was nine and I caught my mother having a bath when she shouldn't have been.

So even if I could stand up and walk into my mother and my father's bedroom, I wouldn't. Too risky. Not allowed.

Instead, I crawled over to the window and opened it. The rain had stopped. Outside smelled of mud. I put my head out and tried to scrape in some air, but it was hard. My shoulders were stiff, held high. My hands were clenched. My body was no longer my own. It was out of control. Bleeding one end. Unable to breathe the other. Hot, tight, frantic everywhere in between. I was crying. Scrape, scrape. I slid down the wall under the window. Well, not slid. It was stiffer than slid. I bashed down the wall under the window in stages, like a puppet made of rocks.

Thud.

"Rachel, Rachel!"

My mother was angry with me. I should have asked for help. If I had gone to their room and knocked on the door and asked for help, then I may have gotten to the doctor in time. I wouldn't need an injection of adrenaline, or need ten days in hospital with a mask over my face, or need to smell of marmite and drink at least one jug of water a day, or need to long for afternoon visits and meat pies with baked beans.

Have I mentioned I hate hospitals? Nurses scare me. Doctors scare me. Patients scare me. I spend the whole time wondering if I'll ever be allowed out again, waiting for the doctor to do his rounds and say, "Rachel Ross? Ah, yes…"—looking at his notes—"this is the one who will never get out again, who will spend the rest of her life in this bed, with this mask on her face, with a view of an incongruous housing estate overlooking a black wind-swept ocean."

I'd spend my days dreading the doctor's words ("No, Rachel, we'd like to keep a wee eye on you for a bit longer"); dreading the nurse's checks ("You need to drink this entire jug of water or you'll be on a drip, Rachel!"); dreading the arrival or removal of other patients ("She died last night, Rachel."—Right there beside me!); and waiting for my mother and my father to visit, which they always did, religiously, like everything else they did.

It was probably this fear that made me decide to be a doctor.

Inside, I felt destined to spend my life in hospital. So, I figured, let me be the one with the coat. Or, if I'm the one in the bed, let me know and understand what's happening to me. Let me have some control. I liked to be in control.

But I wasn't this time. I was lying in bed, clueless, powerless.

My mother attempted to hug me and was like, "You're all elbows, Rachel." Apparently I wasn't much of a hugger. All stiff and bony.

"Pray to the lord for common sense," she said.

To the power of infinity. Amen.

• • •

There was an old lady in my ward. Her name was Joan and she smiled all the time.

"I think you have common sense," she said after my mother left the ward. "I think you're a very lovely girl. And you're going to get better really soon."

She died the following day. Not in her sleep, like the one who carked it last time, but noisily, behind the curtains, yelling *No! No! Please help me!* then making noises like someone was strangling her. The curtains opened an hour later. I closed my eyes while they took her away.

There was a young girl called Bronte in the bed opposite mine. She was fourteen and talked nonstop and her mother brought her whatever she wanted, including photographs of her boyfriend and bags and bags of those Italian chocolates with nuts in the middle.

"Have you had sex?" she asked when old lady Joan had finally left the building.

"None of your business."

She said, "I have. But don't tell anyone."

"I never tell secrets," I said, which was true. I didn't like it when people a) told me their own secrets or b) told me other people's. But if they did, I never mentioned it again, because it was personal, private, and would almost always harm someone if passed on.

In fact, I'd had a reputation for secret-keeping on the island since Louisa MacDonald stole a ten pound note from a cheese stall at the monthly farmer's market and she saw me see her do it. After that, she told me all her secrets. Most of them were pretty lame, like she cheated on a math test and put dog shit in a bag and set it on fire at her ex's doorstep. Then, one by one, people started trusting me with stuff I wish they hadn't, accosting me at the playground or after church and whispering into my ear things that I didn't want to hear, and certainly didn't want to repeat. *Keep quiet* was my motto.

"This is Dean." Bronte showed me a photo of the boy in question. He was at least three years older than her. He was in Speedos, banana hammocks. He made me need my mask.

I sucked the steroid-infused air from my nebulizer.

I had some other visitors during my stay. Mandy and Louisa came by twice with homework, candy, and magazines, and my father came alone one evening and held my hand.

21

"Are you happy?" he said, tearing up.

Retard.

• • •

When I got out of hospital, my mother made me lie in bed for three days before letting me hang out with Mandy.

The Grogans lived on the farm next to ours. They had more land, and better land. They had sheep, pigs, horses, and cattle. They had four girls. Mrs. Grogan wore designer clothes bought on the biannual shopping sprees in Glasgow as well as shipped up four times a year from a designer friend in London. She asked me to call her Aunty Jen, which I did, even though it felt bizarre 'cause she was no more my aunty than my father was. She baked, every day, and entered her perfectly sized, exceptionally straight carrots into the church fair each year. She always won and always wrote about the fair (her win) in daft newspaper articles that my father always published because Mrs. Grogan was my Aunty Jen. The articles went something like this:

BEST CARROTS ON RECORD!

Mrs. Jennifer Grogan won first prize at the annual island show last Saturday for carrots described by judges as "the best carrots on record!"

"It's nothing," Mrs. Jennifer Grogan said. "Just good luck, hard work, and a certain oneness with nature."

My mother didn't like Aunty Jen. She'd come over to our farm at least once a day with baking that reminded my mother that she was a crap baker, homegrown tomatoes that reminded my mother she was a crap gardener, and tales about her livestock that reminded my mother she was a crap farmer. Whenever Aunty Jen left, my mother would shut the door behind her, sigh heavily, and stare into space.

I liked her, though. She was a normal parent. When Mandy had sleepovers, which she did at least once a term, her mother would totally leave us alone except to yell at us ("Girls, we are trying to sleep! Turn that music down! Mandy, didn't I tell you to switch those straighteners off when you're finished? You'll burn the house down!"). Unlike my mum, who—during the one sleepover I'd had; I would never host another one—was always popping her head in my room and smiling and asking us in a soft voice if we were all right and if we wanted anything. *So* embarrassing.

The Grogans were in the process of sending all four of their big-chested, perfectly groomed blondies to Aberfeldy Halls for their final year at school. Don't know why they bothered, really. The two who'd been already had only just scraped through. One was working in a bar in Aberdeen. One was in beauty school in Inverness (which was tougher than you might imagine, apparently).

• • •

I walked over our paddocks, through the fence I'd fixed just before my asthma attack, and across the Grogans' fields to their huge white two-story house (all houses on the island were white). The journey from ours to theirs only took about ten minutes cross-country, but it was like being transported from the world of the peasant to the world of the landlord. They had stables with horses and all. I hadn't been outside for a long time, and there seemed to be too much light and air. Everything was wobbly, especially me.

"You get to go into town on Fridays and do whatever you want," Mandy told me as she showed off her gorgeous blue and maroon uniform.

We were in her attic bedroom, which had a blue-tiled private bathroom, a double bed with one of those flouncy white things flowing down from the ceiling, a computer, and a telly with satellite. It was so unfair.

"Marg used to meet her boyfriend from Baltyre Academy and they'd go down the river," she said. Marg was her beauty-therapist older sister.

"You get to smoke on the fire escapes," she told me, holding up her gold handbag-esque schoolbag. "There's about a thousand butts at the bottom and the teachers don't say anything. You get to go to ceilidhs twice a year." She started showing off her new white duvet cover and weekend clothes. "Marg says Baltyre Academy boys are good looking and can dance."

I walked back to peasant-ville. My legs were working better now, but everything still felt otherworldly. Our small white house, in particular, seemed to shift and blur in the distance. As usual, a feeling of dread settled in my tummy as I approached home. I would have to go inside. I would have to eat dinner at our quiet table. I would have to sleep in my small room with no flouncy white thing, no computer, no private bathroom, and no satellite.

I had to find a way to go to Aberfeldy Halls.

• • •

"You need straight As to get into Medicine at Oxford," I said to my parents that night over roast lamb and roast potatoes and broccoli.

My father said, "And why would you want to get into Medicine at Oxford?" He always answered a question with a question, using as many words from the original question as possible.

"So I can be proud of myself," I said sadly, knowing it was never going to happen.

Why would they understand my ambitions? Neither of them had ambitions anymore, not like in the old days. My father had been a high-flying world affairs journalist for a national newspaper. He'd traveled all over the world to report on big (mostly tragic) events. He used to whistle nonstop. Now he ran the local newspaper and wrote about ferry cancellations and trapped sheep. He never whistled. My mother had been a fund-raiser for a big charity. She used to wear gorgeous designer clothes that made her look like a French movie star. Now she dressed in old jeans and woolen jumpers. Now she stared into space and sighed heavily while her brain crunched like a computer that's slowed by a virus, and tried to look after some of the sheep my father reported on. They'd been proud of themselves once. It hadn't gotten them anywhere.

• • •

A week after my release from hospital, my mother and my father dropped me off at the village dance.

"We'll pick you up at 10 p.m.," my father said. "Wait with Mrs. Grogan inside the foyer until your mum comes in to collect you."

I wore my fave outfit: denim mini skirt, silver top, silver shoes. I looked good. But my nose was red and my eyes were slightly intense, and I had three pimples on my chin and no matter how long I blow-dried my thick, wavy, brown hair, it didn't flatten it the way Mandy's ceramic straighteners did hers.

Mandy and I were embarrassingly early. We sat on two seats near the DJ, watching as the lights dimmed enough for the town's Populars to make their entrance.

"Did you meet a girl called Bronte in hospital?" Mandy asked.

"Yeah."

"She's a total slut."

"That's not nice."

Mandy was like, "Did you not notice her stomach?"

"No."

"Eight months. Maybe some boy called Dean, maybe not. Her parents are putting her under house arrest. They're never letting her out again."

She was about to volunteer more unwanted info when John walked up to us.

"Dance?" he said. He had very bad low-cut jeans that revealed two inches of his gray boxers, and a tight black T-shirt.

"Thought you chucked me."

"Well, I'm picking you up again, aren't I?" he said.

We danced then John went and got some Irn-Bru and sat beside me in the corner.

• • •

About an hour later, I found myself sitting on a toilet seat in the bathroom.

"Rachel!"

I opened the door to the toilet cubicle and peered out. It was my mother.

"Come with me." She grabbed my hand and dragged me from the ladies' toilets and through the dance floor (everyone stopped and looked) and through the foyer (everyone stopped and looked) and into the car out the front.

Mrs. Grogan had seen me and John. She'd called my mother.

What followed turned out to be the best week of my life.

I was grounded.

No telly. No phone. No pals. No reading.

But it was still the best week of my life because at the end of it, my mother and my father sat me down at the dining table and said, "Darling, you're going to Aberfeldy Halls."

CHAPTER THREE

My mother and my father drove me to Aberfeldy Halls a few weeks after the school dance. I'd been so excited I hadn't gone out at all since that night. Besides, there was no use risking another asthma attack, no use risking the need to hide out in a toilet. I'd bought books online, read as many of them as I could, and packed and re-packed my suitcase about one hundred times.

Finally, the day came to leave.

My father edged our four-wheel drive up the ramp and onto the ferry. It was an elderly no-nonsense carrier that was mostly for cars, but there was a thin room with graffiti-covered tables and chairs to sit in for the hour it took to sway our way to the other side. The windows were round and tiny: fogged on the inside and obscured by horizontal rain on the out, so you could hardly see anything. This was the beat-up, two-door, no-central-steering, Ford Fiesta of ferries. I'd always hated it, from the day we first drove our car onto it, waving good-bye to the real world. But this time I loved it. It was taking me away. After an hour in water purgatory, we would drive off it and onto the mainland and freedom.

After docking, the drive took two and a half hours. I looked out the back of the car window as the island disappeared from view, thinking *good riddance floating prison, good riddance.* We drove past hills, more hills—nothing jagged, just rolling and peaceful. No trees at first, then some, then flowers on grass, and flowers in tubs on quaint riverside cottage verandas.

Aberfeldy Halls stood on the edge of the pretty market town of Aberfeldy. There were the usual shops in the village strip: butcher, hairdresser, pub/café, newsagent, pub/supermarket, post office, pub/Indian takeaway, chemist, fish and chip shop, pub. After the small line of shops was a line of quaint stone, terraced cottages set back no more than two feet from the road. Out the front of one of the cottages sat an unmanned trestle table with gingham-topped pots of homemade jam. A jar of coins indicated the high level of honesty the villagers expected from their customers. Further on from the cottages were large, detached houses with turrets and meticulously pruned hedges.

The village ended with a thin stone bridge over a fast, deep, salmon-filled river. Ten meters beyond the river, an iron gate on the left displayed the words "Aberfeldy Halls." My limbs were numb, my heart pounding, as we drove through the gates, up the 500-meter driveway towards the old sandstone mansion. Once, this building might have been considered imposing: the sort of place Jane Austen's wealthier characters would live in. It was a house, originally, but the rich bloke who owned it sold it in the 1980s, and it became a private boarding school. Since then, new buildings had been added—the mostly glass office and dining building to the right, which was connected by a thin, covered walkway to the four-story pebble-dashed dorms, and the gym, nestled in behind the playing fields to the left. Behind the dorms was a beautiful thick wood. The wood and the new buildings made the whole place comfortable. It wasn't imposing at all. It was dynamic, beautiful, and inviting.

"You get to drink white wine in the woods," Mandy had told me. "You get to hide there during study time and have secret rendezvous with boys from Baltyre Academy."

• • •

Miss Rose met us at reception in the office building. She introduced herself as the third-floor matron, but "matron" seemed the wrong label for her entirely. With trendy short light brown hair and a flowing multi-colored hippie skirt, she oozed all things un-matronly: approachability, tranquility, kindness. She was around the same age as my mother, but she was prettier.

Also, every second thing she said did not involve "the good lord." I liked her immediately. She welcomed me with a hug.

Miss Rose walked us through the classrooms, all of which were located in the original manor. Despite the high decorative ceilings, the rooms were clean and crisp like the year's first notebook. On the top floor there was a theatre and an impressive art department. The store was in the basement across from the Church of Scotland chapel, where you could light a fake candle for fifty pence.

The track and the fields were as groomed as Mandy's mum. There was a sparking new gym with basketball courts and a pool nestled in behind them. This was a school for rich kids, I realized. And I wondered, for the first time ever, how on earth my parents could afford to send me here. One day, maybe I'd ask them. But not now. Guilt was not welcome now.

Back in the dining hall at the back of the office building, Miss Rose explained about meal times. Breakfast was from 7:00 to 8:00, lunch from 12:30 to 1:30, tea from 6:00 to 7:00. As she talked, I looked out the large glass windows towards the pebble dash dorms, desperate to walk out along the thin concrete walkway to my cubicle.

Oh sweet cubicle.

Probably not very different in size from a prison cell, made from dark wood, with a large sliding door that didn't lock and walls that didn't quite reach the ceiling. Mine was second from the fire escape on the third floor (Right). Each of the four floors had a Right and a Left, with a shower block in the middle, a small communal kitchen with a microwave and kettle, two rows of twenty cubicles either side, and a fire escape at each end. I looked out my new cubicle window to see if it was true about the cigarette butts at the bottom of the fire escapes (it was—must've been at least 1,000), then shielded my mother and my father from doing the same, or else they'd have driven me straight home again.

Please go! Please get out! My mother and my father were asking about nurses (there was one) and nebulizers (there was one) and Sunday observance (they would make sure I attended the local free church on Sundays) and holidays (not compulsory to go home) and phone calls (no mobiles allowed, please use the pay phone in the hall on the ground floor; if someone phones you, we will call you over the loudspeaker) and *please go. Leave me alone. Let me sit in my room, with my suitcase and my red duvet and my desk. Leave me to greet Mandy Grogan and Louisa MacDonald who may arrive any moment. To write my name on the new notebooks I bought from one-eyed Mrs. Crookston at the village shop (Thank you, I'd said to her, looking straight into it).*

"Right then," Miss Rose said. "I'll leave you to say your good-byes."

"Good-bye," my mother said. She seemed a tad tearful. I'd not seen her tearful in a long time.

"Good-bye," my father said. He was always a tad tearful.

"Good-bye," I said, taking the bible my mother handed me and watching as they walked down three flights and across the walkway towards the dining hall.

I admit: I was a bit upset seeing them go. They seemed so bereft, so ill at ease in each other's company.

But the melancholy only lasted for as long as I could still see them. Soon as I couldn't, I did a silent-scream-while-jumping-up-and-down-a-bit. I was in heaven. Not by myself in the middle of damp nowhere, praying on a hardwood floor. Not listening to teachers who knew less than I did. In *heaven*. Putting my favorite bright red duvet cover on my bed then bouncing on it. Peeking out my window. Pushing at the fire escape door. Checking out the toilets. The cupboards on the landing. Reading the rules for the television room directly underneath my cubicle. Exploring the hobby rooms on the second floor—a bright sewing room, a messy arts and crafts room, a darkroom that was no longer in use since the onset of digital cameras.

"Submissions for ideas on the use of this room are welcome," Miss Rose had told me when we'd passed it earlier on, pointing out a sheet pinned to the door. Already three suggestions had appeared: group study, music room, and internet café. I turned the key in the door and snooped inside—the room was empty, nothing special.

Back in my cubicle, I lay out my laptop, a notebook, a pen, a pencil, and a calculator on my desk

My own world. My own space.

This was the beginning. I would make things happen here. I would make myself proud, my parents proud. I would work hard, be good, the best, the top. Small fish in a big pond? Not me. A big one in a big one.

The beginning.

A noise.

Miss Rose again. Another mother. Another father. A girl, sliding the door to the cubicle beside me. A new friend perhaps? Someone to giggle with in the shower rooms? Someone to chat with before going to bed? Someone to learn from, study with?

I listened to the good-byes (*I love you! Write to us! Take care, eat sensibly…you know…yes? Enjoy it, won't you! I don't want to leave you! Love you, love you, bye!*).

Knock knock.

I slid my door open.

"This is your neighbor," Miss Rose said. "Amelia O'Donohue, this is Rachel Ross."

"Pleased to meet you," Amelia O'Donohue said.

"You too," I said.

We shook hands. She had thick, long, wavy hair, unlike everyone else who flattened theirs to look like brown paper. She wore a shirt with the collar up, and a sleeveless jumper on top that was so small the bottom of her shirt hung out from underneath it. Her eyes were the largest, brownest eyes I'd ever seen. Her skin was the clearest, brownest skin I'd ever seen. She had big boobs. She was slim, not skinny like me. I was so skinny my father sometimes put his fingers round my wrist and lifted my arm up and laughed. She had the latest high-waisted shorts and cool shoes and very white, straight teeth.

"You're the first to arrive! Early birds! Best of friends, I can tell," Miss Rose said. "I'm going to leave you to chatter and unpack your paraphernalia."

Miss Rose said words like *paraphernalia*. What a hoot.

We listened to her walk down the hall and down the first flight of stairs and then Amelia's expression changed from fake-smiley to snarly and in a very posh English accent she said, "No coming into my room. No asking me for stuff. No touching my stuff. No geeky music. Any questions?"

"No. I think I've got…"

Didn't get a chance to say "it." Amelia O'Donohue had exited my cubicle with a spectacularly loud bang of my sliding door and entered her own, where she proceeded to plug in her iPod and play very loud music that I had never heard before but was definitely not geeky.

Obviously from a big English city, maybe even London. She probably went to clubs on weekends and bought ready-mixed Bacardi and Cokes from the liquor store without even flinching.

I did a silent-scream-while-jumping-up-and-down-a-bit.

This place was amazing! So amazing I found myself kneeling beside my very own bed on my very own hardwood floor and praying voluntarily, "Dear god, even though I don't believe in you, thank you for sending me here. I will make you proud. I will thank you every day. And sorry for my sins. And god bless my mother and god bless my father. To the power of infinity. Amen."

CHAPTER FOUR

The dorms swarmed with sixteen- and seventeen-year-old girls from exotic places like the west end of Glasgow and Inverness. They all seemed to know each other or have stuff in common to talk about like music and reality television. They all had treats like cupcakes with coconut-covered chocolate icing on top and large allowances to go to McDonald's on Fridays and to the local shop after school. They all had mobile phones (even though you weren't supposed to—indeed I seemed to be the only girl at school who'd followed the rules). I wandered round checking everyone out and introducing myself ("Hello, I'm Rachel Ross, pleased to meet you. What do you want to do at university?").

"One thing at a time, eh Raylene!" said the first. (She was a bit tough and scary up close—had thick eyeliner on and at least two coats of foundation—so I didn't correct her. Raylene would do for now.)

"Engineering," said the second, "at Cambridge, but if

it's St. Andrews, it's St. Andrews, but I'm confident it'll be Cambridge," then she buzzed off to check out the darkroom on the second floor.

"What? I dunno. Got a smoke?" said the third. She'd tried to hide it with cover up, but I could see she'd been crying.

"I'm not going to university until the government down south abolishes fees," said the fourth in her northern English accent, before placing an antiracism poster on the notice board on the landing.

"Get a life dick wad," said the fifth, sliding her cubicle door shut.

Oh delicious, eclectic new world!

I finally found Mandy Grogan's room on the fourth floor (Left) to discover she was next door to her big sister's best mate's little sister and that they'd headed down to the woods together.

I walked out of the dorm building and round the back, where huge, thick conifers padded the hills and traipsed along one of the forest tracks. Down at the very bottom was a derelict wooden shack. I could hear noises coming from inside, but felt too scared and too shy to open the door and see if it was Mandy and her new friend. I returned to the dorms to seek out Louisa, who was in the television room on the second floor. Five other girls, including Amelia O'Donohue, were in there with her.

"Hi, this is Rachel," she said, introducing me to her new friends. "She's a brain box, and totally the one to tell secrets to…never tell, do you Rach?"

"Hi," I said, wishing there was somewhere for me to sit. The ads were on, and the girls were talking about cute teachers, Baltyre boys, and what to do in town on Friday evenings. The three sofas were full, so I sat on the arm of the couch Louisa was on. It was very uncomfortable. For a start, Louisa didn't even move her arm to give me a bit more space. My bottom started feeling numb and I didn't know where to put my hands.

"What do you want to do at university?" I asked the girl next to Louisa.

"Rachel, not everybody cares so much about university," Louisa answered. The girl I'd asked hadn't even bothered responding. The adverts had finished and some show about murders had started. I think she may have even rolled her eyes.

I could feel my arms getting bigger. I decided to fold them. This made balancing on the arm of the sofa quite difficult.

"What's this?" I asked anyone who might answer.

"*Crime Scene Investigation*," said Mandy, who was sitting next to Amelia O'Donohue. Amelia was watching the show with immense concentration. "Shh!" Amelia said. "I bet they're gonna find his DNA on the cheese grater."

The next few minutes were spent deciding how to leave the room with dignity. Should I pretend I had something exciting to do and tell everyone before flouncing out? Should I say "See ya!" cheerfully, then go? Or should I fidget and sweat, red-faced, before unfolding my arms and skulking numb-bummed out the door? I went for the latter.

If Mandy and Louisa were ignoring me a bit, I didn't mind. Like me, they were excited to be here. Anyway, I had longer-term goals than popularity and fun in mind. I was at Aberfeldy Halls to pave the way for a lifelong escape from the island.

• • •

It was dinner time. Miss Rose announced it over the intercom: *Girls, the bell is about to ring for supper.* I headed over the walkway and grabbed a seat at one of the huge round tables. Mandy and Louisa joined me a few minutes later.

"Guess what!" Mandy always started conversations this way, and I always made at least seven silly guesses before she coughed up. It was a game we'd played since we were little. This time, she didn't wait for my guesses (which would have been something like: You found £10,000! Or: Your father is gay!). "This girl Aimee from my floor," Mandy said, "is like so cool and sweet and she has an iPod with the Jonas Brothers on and a bright pink portable battery-operated dock and we played it down in the woods in that shack and she brought a whole suitcase of cigarettes and she took one of them down there too. Louisa had three."

"Did you inhale?" I asked Louisa.

"Aye, course."

"The telly on second has satellite and Amelia O'Donohue..." Mandy said.

"She is too cool," Louisa interjected.

"I know...anyhow she recorded the whole second series of *CSI* and we're all gonna meet up after lights out and watch them and see who can guess whodunit first."

"Who's *all?*" I asked.

"Amelia, and Ally from Wick—she is so funny. And a group from Glasgow who all know each other already from this nightclub they go to."

"What's the shack like?" I asked Mandy.

"Unreal. There's writing all over: Jennifer pulled Mick here 20-03-2005, drawings of boys' bits, stuff like that. Someone's left condoms in there. Under an old mattress. Apparently people shag there all the time. Oh guess what?" I opened my mouth to guess, but there was no time..."Aimee's gonna have a midnight feast in my room! Knock three times, very quietly..."

To my surprise, Amelia O'Donohue sat down opposite me.

She was so stunning that everyone at the table stopped talking. We were in the presence of tremendous beauty, humbled by her eyes and by her expensive designer puff skirt, thick belt, and very unbuttoned silk shirt. We all deferred to her, waiting for her to initiate conversation, hanging on every word she said. In the end, all she said was: "This food is disgusting," and "This place is like a prison."

The two choices for dinner were a large, round, tomato-soaked meatball (I heard Amelia O'Donohue calling it an abortion as she asked for two extra), and a large pasty. The chef, a good-looking forty-something, served the main course onto our plates. Miss Rose chatted and giggled with him as she garnished the plates with a selection of vegetables. They looked good together, I thought, but any ideas of matchmaking were ruined by the gleaming wedding ring visible on the chef's finger. I chose the meatball, but I couldn't eat it after the nickname Amelia had given it.

• • •

That night, I was hanging my clothes in the built-in wardrobe with my flannelette pajamas on, when my door smashed open to reveal Amelia O'Donohue (in a pink silk teddy-style nightie).

"I need your help," she said, sliding the door shut.

"Okay."

"My boyfriend's on the fire escape," she said.

"Oh my god!"

"Shh! God's sake…I've rigged the door so the alarm doesn't go off. But you cover for me, yeah?"

"How?"

"Don't let anyone go out to smoke and don't let anyone in my cubicle. If anyone asks, say I'm asleep."

I didn't get a chance to say anything. She'd already checked her hair in the mirror and left.

I could see the fire escape from my window. There were no external lights on, but the hall lights lit it up. I opened my window a tad and looked out. A boy of about seventeen was leaning against the metal banister. He'd obviously spent a long time on his asymmetrical light brown hair. Each strand was placed with perfect, edgy randomness. Amelia came out from the fire escape door and joined him (still in her teddy!). Can I say/think/write what happened next? Is it too rude? Too rude to hint that Amelia must have had very sore knees afterwards?

"Amelia!"

Oh no. Someone was looking for Amelia.

I slammed my window shut, ran out my door, and shielded Amelia's room with my arms.

"She's asleep!" I said.

The girl was dressed in the same nightie as Amelia but in a different color. She had perfectly flat, highlighted hair. And makeup. At bed time! Glittery gold eye shadow, at least three thick coats of mascara, which made her short lashes clumpy to be honest, and bright pink, clown-like blusher that Mandy had told me was "the thing" these days. She turned up her lip and said, "Who are you?"

"Rachel Ross. Amelia asked me to make sure no one interrupts her. She's exhausted."

"Since when are you friends with Amelia?" she said, looking at my pajama ensemble.

"Dunno."

She was like, "Whatever, tell her Tanya needs to talk to her urgently." (Tanya with a poncy aah…Taahnya.) Obviously from the city. She probably ate avocado and pine nuts with multicolored lettuce.

The lights went out at 10 p.m., and Amelia had still not come back inside. I lay in bed waiting for the fire escape door to clink shut, for hers to slide open, to hear her lying down in her bed, her head only centimeters from mine though the thin wall dividing us.

Finally, must have been an hour after lights out, the fire

escape door clicked. There were footsteps, then a door sliding open. But it wasn't Amelia's. It was mine.

"Anyone come looking?" Amelia said.

"Just Taahnya. Said she needs to talk to you urgently."

"Slap my cheek then pull my nose then say: *If I tell, I'll go to hell.*"

I was like, "What?"

"Slap my cheek then pull my nose then say: *If I tell, I'll go to hell.*"

"I never tell people's secrets. I promise. I have a reputation for it back home. Ask Mandy and Louisa, they'll tell you it's true."

"Who the fudge is Mandy and Louisa?" Crikey, she was so cool she said fudge like all the time and made a point of not remembering nobodies. "Slap my cheek then pull my nose then say it."

"But you can't send me to hell and anyway I don't believe in it."

"I'll make your life so crap you'll believe in it. Do it."

So I closed my eyes and slapped her right cheek.

"Ow! Not so hard."

I opened my eyes a bit and slapped her other (not red) cheek more softly and then pulled her nose for three seconds...

"That's long enough! Jeez..." she said.

I let go and said, "If I tell, I'll go to hell."
Amelia nodded then left my room.

CHAPTER FIVE

I set my alarm clock for ten to twelve and woke up wondering where I was. After a couple of seconds the wonderful truth dawned on me. I wasn't with my misery-soaked parents in the middle of nowhere, the sea crashing against the rocks across the road, the wind howling through the emptiness of our treeless farm. I was in the wondrous Aberfeldy Halls. I got out of bed and tiptoed along the hall and up the stairs to the fourth floor. I counted the cubicles as I made my way to Mandy's room for our midnight feast, then knocked three times very quietly on the fourteenth on the right. I could hear two girls giggling. Eventually, the door slid open.

Mandy, Louisa, and a girl called Aimee were sitting on the bed eating cupcakes.

"You'll never guess what we heard," Mandy said.

"You can't tell her," Aimee said.

"This is Rachel Ross," Mandy said, "the most trustworthy girl in the world. No matter how hard you try, she won't tell you a thing. It's abnormal, actually. I've told Rach absolutely all my juicy secrets and she's never told anyone."

"Really, like what?" Aimee said.

I didn't say anything.

Aimee was like, "So you really keep secrets?"

"There's no need to tell me if you'd rather not."

"Oh, but you'll die! Y'know the girl who wears the same clothes as Amelia O'Donohue?"

"Aye, Taahnya…"

"That's the one. Taahnya Scot. Posh bitch from Edinburgh. Anyways, guess what she had…"

I didn't guess.

"An abortion!"

My lack of response didn't please them.

"Can you believe that? Her big sister told my big sister that's why her parents sent her here."

"Can I have a cupcake?" I said.

The girls told me loads of other gossip. There were lesbians on their floor, apparently. With nose rings. Squelchy noises had been heard at around 10:50 that very night. The culprits were called Vanessa and Jill.

Suddenly, a door slammed somewhere close by. The three of us shut our mouths and stopped breathing, listening as footsteps pounded past the cubicle, then back again, then back again, then stopped dead, then the door slid open slowly.

It was Miss Jamieson, the fourth floor matron. Each floor's matron slept in full height lockable cubicles situated beside the bathrooms.

"To bed now, girls!" she said, more calmly than I'd have expected considering her grim demeanor. She had a very thin face and cheeks that caved into an unfortunate jaw.

"I understand your excitement tonight," she said, "but I catch you again you'll be on toilet duties for a month."

There were toilet duties?

I hardly slept that night. ALO (Dorm speak for After Lights Out), girls quieted down for a while, before coming to life again, confident that the matrons would be asleep. They tiptoed into each other's rooms to eat, chat, giggle. They snuck down to the television room to watch scary movies on low volume. They smoked on the fire escape. All of which contributed to a hum of ad hoc noises that made sleep impossible. To make things worse, the clock beside the cupboards made an eerie buzzing sound every hour, and I found myself waiting for the next one, hour by hour, till Real Radio played at 7 a.m. to wake us for breakfast.

"Morning, Miss Rose," I said as I walked back from the shower room to my cubicle.

"Morning, Rachel," she said, smiling. Poor thing, living in a dorm full of girls. It must get lonely, I thought.

Ouch. Taahnya had grabbed me by the arm as Miss Rose turned to walk away. She was dragging me down the corridor and into my room.

"What are you doing?" I asked when she pushed me down onto my bed.

She was like, "What did Amelia tell you about me?"

"Nothing."

"I'm going to count to three and if you haven't told me, then I'm going to punch you on the arm till you do."

"She hasn't told…"

"*One…*"

"Me anything…"

"*Two…*"

"Really!"

"*Three.*"

"Ow!"

She'd kept her word and had punched me really hard on the arm.

"Now tell me or I'll punch you twice this time."

"She hasn't told…"

Punch. Punch.

"Jesus!"

"One more chance, then I'll just keep punching."

"One…Two…Three…"

As she punched, I tried to tell her that I was being completely honest…Amelia had said nothing…

"What about the other girls?"

"No one's told me anything…" I said, sacrificing honesty for discretion.

It was killing me. My arm was numb.

"Well…I suppose you are telling the truth," she said, shaking her red hand and leaving the room.

• • •

I loved my uniform, even though my mother had ordered it secondhand from some scabby shop in Perth. The skirt was long, pleated, and thick: a blue and maroon tartan. White shirt, blue tie, maroon cardigan, maroon blazer, tights, black shoes. I looked *official*. Posh even. When I got to breakfast, I was surprised at how different the girls could make a standard uniform look. Amelia O'Donohue had fashioned her tie into a loose, short, massive knot. Her top two buttons were undone. Her collar was up. Her white shirt hung undone from underneath her tight V-neck jumper, and she'd discarded the mandatory blazer.

While I queued at the huge, round, toaster, which the chef oversaw, Miss Rose at his side, I realized word had somehow gotten around that I was *the* person to tell stuff to. I was waiting for my whole-grain toast to be handed over when a girl with a ponytail and a really short skirt whispered, "I fancy the gym teacher, Mr. Burns."

"Really?" I whispered back, not sure what else to say. I'd never met the girl with the ponytail, nor Mr. Burns. But when I did—my third lesson was PE—I understood. He was quite young—around 25 perhaps—with dark curly hair, stubble, large muscles, and a nice manner.

"Does anyone want to be an Olympic athlete?" he asked.

A few girls put their hands up, including the girl with the ponytail.

"Good. And why not? Live your dreams. Be the best you can. Now ladies, three laps of the field! Except the girls who put their hands up…you do five…"

"Mr. Bu…urns," the girl with the ponytail flirted.

"Now, now, Olympic athletes never moan! They embrace!" he said, putting his hand on her shoulder and pushing her off with a smile.

Every period excited me. The classrooms all had interactive whiteboards which communicated with electronic pens and our own personal laptops.

My English teacher, Catherine (she asked us to call her Catherine!), began by writing two lines on the whiteboard…

A poem should be palpable and mute
As a globed fruit

"What do you think this means?" she asked. Unlike in my old class, almost everyone put their hands up. Back home, questions had been answered with the communal sliding of bums down chairs.

"It means poetry is more than words." This came from a girl called Viv Metstein, an unruly chubster with scuffed shoes.

"Good, Viv. Anyone else?" My head, hair and all, had suddenly become boiling hot. *I know the words on the board are fantastic*, I thought, *but I dunno why. God, what does it mean? Don't ask me. Please.*

"I think it means you can almost taste a good poem." Louisa said this. Louisa was good at English.

"Totally!" Catherine said, before glancing around for her next genius. "It's Rachel, isn't it?" She smiled directly at me. Oh shite. How had she managed to remember our names already? "What do you think?"

"Um…" The heat was now having a throbbing party on my

cheeks. "Is it like, tempting, delicious, beckoning?" Was this correct? Was this silly?

"Yes! Outstanding. Girls, this year I just know we are going to have a love affair with words."

I blew out the heat with a loud sigh, then beamed. I stayed like this all day.

Teachers who loved teaching! Pupils who loved learning! It was everything I hoped it would be.

Biology was particularly fun. The teacher—Mr. Kaw Sharma from Kashmir—was passionate about his work, and he made us buzz as he talked about how oxytocin stimulates uterine contraction during childbirth. I was so engrossed that I didn't notice Amelia O'Donohue leaving a note on my desk that said: "You're on watch again tonight."

After school, we returned to the dorms for a wee rest and our first study period. I was just in the zone with trigonometry when two girls knocked on my cubicle. The first, a thin pale girl called Lucy, burst into tears when I told her I was indeed trustworthy and if she needed to talk, I would be happy to listen. Turned out, her aunty had tried to kill herself in the summer. She was worried she might try again. And succeed. Could she turn to me if this happened? The second girl was a rosy-cheeked, Girl-Guide type called Roberta. "I don't want anyone else to know," she chirped, "but Mum says it's a good idea to have a friend to talk to about it. I've got lupus, see. I'm being eaten alive."

"I'm Jennifer Buckley," said the next girl in line.

"Hi, Jennifer, and what seems to be the problem?" I had taken to doctor-speak like a duck to water.

"I miss my cat," she said, showing me a photograph of a ginger tabby then bursting into tears. "She licks my toes and I know it sounds gross but it makes me feel better. Without Mercy I feel like crying all the time."

If people wanted to tell me things, should I try and stop them? Should I stop them unloading? Leave them to ferment? Or should I ease their burden by taking at least part of it and hiding it inside me? Did I have a choice? It seemed to me that I didn't. It seemed to me that I was the only person who truly believed that if you break a confidence, if you let loose a dangerous truth, you may indeed be damned forever.

CHAPTER SIX

Each day, the girls, the teachers, and the buildings became more and more familiar. By the end of the first month, I could hardly imagine the outside world. Here, everything was simple and everything was decided for you. The only things that could impede study were friendships and homesickness, and I did not suffer from either of them. I politely declined midnight feasts, sneaky cigarettes, and basketball clubs, preferring to work at my desk and get a good night's sleep. I ate well—no lamb, thank god—and became particularly fond of cauliflower cheese, which I'd not eaten before. The chef said he'd never known a girl to come back three times for vegetables. I felt positive and purposeful. The feeling of dread which used to loom as I neared my croft home had disappeared, replaced by stomach-churning excitement at practice tests for math, English essays, and physics assignments. Throughout that first month, girls continued to come to my room and tell me things, and I didn't mind, except that some of them smelled funny, and most of their problems were about missing home and feeling lonely, which I didn't really understand.

A couple of these sessions stick out in my mind. A girl called Vanessa, with a Mohawk and a nose-piercing, came and said only two sentences: "I'm in love" and "Should I tell the person?"

"If it feels right," I said, recalling that this girl was the alleged fourth-floor lesbian.

She nodded her head, sighed, and left.

Another evening, a girl called Janey Harris came in and fidgeted nervously on the edge of my bed. "I can't tell you, no I can't…It's too awful."

"You don't have to," I reassured her, but before I knew it she'd lifted her shirt to reveal a hairy lump underneath her left arm. I tried to disguise how sick it made me feel. It was a bumpy fur ball, three inches in diameter.

"It's my twin," she said, bursting into tears. "I took it over in Mum's tummy and I absorbed him…Mum says I should just get it removed, but I can't do it. They call it parasitic. I call him James." She stroked it.

Holy fudge, was that a *tooth*?

When she left, I ran to the loos to puke. Gross.

The wee soul.

I suppose I didn't realize it, but I was becoming pretty

isolated. I called my mother and my father once a week from the phone in the hall downstairs. Once, while I was waiting my turn, a girl called Gillie was talking to her boyfriend. She was sitting on her foot and wriggling, obviously desperate to go to the loo but not wanting to say good-bye ("No you hang up, no you, no you…"). When she finally did, we both saw at the same time that she had poo all over her sock. Later, she came to my room and said, "Thank god it was you, Rachel. Someone else might have told everyone."

"Believe me," I said. "I know how important secrets are. I know how destructive it can be to pass private information on. I will never tell anyone about your sock."

I played guard for Amelia O'Donohue, who did ruder and ruder things each time she met her boyfriend on the fire escape. I peeked every now and then. I don't know what she saw in him. There was only one stubble-filled inch between his bottom lip and his neck. He made me feel a little queasy, especially when he was saying, *Oh Amelia, oh, oh.*

I did toilet duties one day every fortnight, which involved scrubbing slimy showers and toothpaste-dotted sinks and brown-stained loos. Once, I had to wait an hour to clean one toilet. As I waited, I heard a disgusting retching sound. Finally, Amelia O'Donohue opened the door.

"What?" she said, startled that I was waiting outside her toilet door. "You stalking me? Creep." She rinsed her mouth in the sink. "It's those bloody abortions."

On Sundays, I begrudgingly went to the church at the other end of the town, as I had promised my folks. This was the only hour of the week that depressed me. Each time, I almost ran back through the village, across the bridge, and up the welcoming driveway to my new home.

I rang John once. Sat nervously over the phone before dialing, then just tapped in the numbers and held my breath. His mother answered the phone.

"Is John there?" I asked.

"He's out," she said.

"Could you leave him a message? Tell him Rachel called. My number's…"

I started reciting the school telephone number, but she interrupted me.

"I'll tell him," she said, and hung up.

I don't know why I phoned him, to be honest. I didn't really like him very much. And the thought of him made me nauseated, like bad prawns from the night before. I never tried phoning again. And he never tried to contact me.

• • •

Gradually, my distaste for the island and the adults who'd imprisoned me there made me sick and angry. After four weeks, something seemed to snap. I couldn't bear to think, hear, or talk about *that* place. So much so that I rang my mother and told her I wouldn't be home till christmas. With the academic year starting in August, the September weekend was the first proper break from school. When we lived in Edinburgh, my mother and my father used to take me camping on the September weekend, as a good-bye to the summer. We'd get all the gear out of the enormous hall cupboard in our bright forty-foot hall and pack the car to breaking point. It always rained, and we always ended up playing monopoly and giggling in the tent, then getting no sleep 'cause my mother snored.

"But we thought we'd go camping..." she began.

"I have a lot of work to do. I'll be fine," I said.

"I want you to come home."

"Why?"

"I'll put your dad on," she said.

"Please come and see us. We miss you," he pleaded.

"I'm sorry, but I'm too busy. It gets me all distracted. Please understand..."

"We love you," he said, trailing off, not saying good-bye. I could almost feel the floppiness of his hands and shoulders.

"Rachel…" My mother had grabbed the phone. "I'm ordering you to come home."

"You can't order me to do anything. I'm almost seventeen."

"I'll say it one last time, Rachel."

I hadn't been defiant like this before. It shocked me, and her. But it felt good. Independence and determination had heated to the boiling point inside me.

"I'm not coming home," I said, and hung up.

And then threw up.

• • •

I decided not to talk to them. I decided not to go to church anymore. I decided to cut them out of my life, for now anyway. Whenever Miss Rose announced over the loudspeaker that there was a phone call for me, I pretended not to hear. Whenever she delivered their letters, I didn't read them. I put them in a shoebox in my cupboard.

When the September weekend came, girls ran out of school to greet their parents. I watched from my cubicle window as happy families left for happy family holidays.

"Your mother is here," Miss Rose said. She was standing at my open door.

"I'm not going," I said.

"You have to talk to her."

"Do I, Miss Rose?"

"Yes," she said.

So I walked out of the dorm building, past the offices, and into the driveway. My mother was in her car, crying. I hadn't ever been away from her so long. She had the same drab clothes on as when I last saw her. The same sad face. But at the same time, she seemed totally new, a stranger.

She wound down her window. "You're not coming home, are you?"

"No."

"What have we done to you to make you so hostile, so *closed-up?*"

"Nothing. I'm sorry. I just want to study, that's all. I don't want *any* distractions. Please understand."

"You know we love you. Can you be kind to us? *Give* a little."

"If you leave me alone for a while."

"What about mid-term break in October?" she said.

"I'll be home for christmas."

She put her hand out of the window, pulled me to her, and kissed my forehead.

• • •

The holiday weekend was really quiet. I worked from 8:00 in the morning till 4:00 in the afternoon, then went for a walk down the driveway, over the river, and through the village.

One afternoon, I was walking past the curry shop. It was right in the center of the strip, with "Balbir's Curry House" written in bright red lettering. Inside looked fabulously un-Scottish— warm and colorful and vibrant, the walls covered in hand-written descriptions of the dozens of curries on offer and in bright photos of Indian palaces and forts. A few café style seats covered in velvety orange material filled the small seating area, but it was mainly a takeaway and the cooking was done behind the counter, in full view of the customers. An Asian boy of around seventeen was opening up.

"Hi there," he said. I only noticed his middle part—large, square shoulders that petered down to a small waist, making an almost perfect triangle. A swimmer, maybe. Boys on the island were not shaped this way. Most of them were at least six inches shorter and had coat hanger shoulders.

I ignored him.

The following afternoon, the same boy was doing the same thing.

"Hi there," he said. This time I noticed the top bit of him. He had curly dark hair, big brown eyes with lashes that girls use fake-lash mascara to achieve, and a wide, infectious, toothy smile.

I ignored him.

Next time he said, "My name's Sammy. What's yours?" I registered his clothes: well-cut jeans, unironed designer T-shirt, freakishly large white trainers. And his voice: second-generation-Scottish, upbeat, sounded like morning birds.

"Rachel," I said, still walking.

"I made you something," he said, running after me with a carrier bag. Inside, was a plastic takeaway container. "My world-famous chicken bhoona. No offense, but you look like you need meat. If I could, I'd put you on a mince drip. You're not a vegetarian?"

"No," I said. "And thanks."

• • •

There was something sunny about this boy Sammy. He wasn't like John, who seemed cloudy and vacant, who'd never managed a conversation with me (other than to ask me to do more than kiss). He was a waste of space. Boys were a waste of space.

Was Sammy?

That night, after I'd read one of the novels for English, I went to the small kitchen on my floor, took the lid off the plastic container Sammy had given me, and put the curry in the microwave. It looked pretty ordinary, like the ones we used to get in Glasgow—all thick and lumpy—but when I took it out of the microwave, several separate smells danced their way from my nostrils to my brain. Garlic, onions, ginger, coriander, tomatoes—each solid, comfortable, and independent, but even better together. I put my fork into one of the large pieces of chicken. Before heating it, I hadn't been looking forward to the meat. I craved meat about as much as I craved the Sabbath. But now, my brain told me there was no time to waste, no time to sit down. I had to taste it. It was unlike anything I'd ever eaten. The chicken was softer than meat should be. It opened itself out, nothing to hide. I ate it slowly, eyes closed, making embarrassing sexual noises as I savored and swallowed. Ahhh. I would think about this for a long time. I would want it again very soon. In fact, I needed to know it was possible. *Now*. I walked out of the dorms, down the driveway, over the river, and into the curry shop.

It was very busy. A line of politely queuing customers waited against the wall and a middle-aged man packaged curries and handed them to the next in line. I could see Sammy's back as he cooked over the burners. He was whistling while cooking. A smiley happy boy, working hard, producing something he loved.

"Can I speak to Sammy for a moment?" I asked the middle-aged man at the counter. He was bald, and the right kind of overweight: soft but not fat. He yelled something in Hindi (I think).

Sammy fiddled with the controls on the cooker, and turned around.

"Hey, Rachel. How was it?" he asked.

"It was…hard to believe. I came to say thank you."

"My pleasure," he said. "Dad, you mind if I take ten?"

The middle-aged man, obviously his father, probably named Balbir, said something in Hindi (I think), which made Sammy laugh, take off his apron, and open the trap door on the counter. "Let's go for a walk," he said.

I was like, "There's no need."

"Of course there's no *need*," he said.

Before we got out of the shop, Sammy had asked me to tell him three surprising things about myself.

"My name's Rachel."

He made a honking sound. "Doesn't count. Not interesting. *And* you already told me that."

"Okay, I come from an island up north…" I was honestly stuck. What was interesting about me? "I can't think of anything else," I said. "You tell me three things first."

"Once I ate a small bowl of red chilies for a dare and had to go to hospital. My first kiss was with Maria Jamieson from

Comrie—she used her tongue and I didn't. And I failed all my standard grades."

We'd reached the driveway.

"Well, Sammy…"

"Sharma."

"Well, Sammy Sharma. You are very forthright. And a very good cook. Do you sell that particular curry all the time?"

"That and many others which are just as good."

"I don't do lamb." I didn't mean this to sound like an order. Or did I?

"Got it. No lamb."

"Well, you'll be seeing me then. But for now, I have to go."

He was like, "You're not getting away that easily. Three things."

"I'm good at keeping secrets. I never lose my temper. And I want to be a doctor."

"Honk! Boring and elusive."

"I am not elusive."

"You're more bottled up than ketchup. If you weren't so cute, I'd have given up already."

"It was nice to meet you," I said, shaking his warm hand and walking up the driveway.

As I made my way towards the school, a bright green convertible stopped beside me.

"Excuse me, do you know when the girls get back?" a boy of around seventeen asked. I recognized him—it was Amelia's asymmetrical-haired fire escape boyfriend. He didn't know me.

"Any time before nine," I said.

"Cheers." He pronounced it chairs. What was Amelia thinking? Blah. I bet after they did it he said things like: "Now woman don't try and tell me you won't savor that for weeks" or "Damn, I forgot to tell Jeeves our Harry can't abide vodka." To add to the whole disgusting ensemble, he had brown goggle eyes and overworked designer stubble.

The girls arrived back at school that night. According to Aimee, Mandy and Louisa headed down the forest track almost as soon as they arrived.

"So how was it?" I asked when the door to the derelict shack was finally opened. I hadn't been inside the shack before. It was for cool people who smoked and shagged and then spray-painted the details on the walls (J has a huge c***, francis is a s***, h and m did it here…twice). I had no business there. But the weekend of almost complete solitude had made me yearn for my old friends.

"Fine," Mandy said, touching her new fringe. She'd had her beautiful curly hair permanently straightened and framed by strand-perfect bangs. It didn't suit her.

"What did you get up to?" I asked.

"Nothing," she said, all distant and monosyllabic. The constant smile I used to love had completely vanished. She'd injected a pout into her lips.

"What about you Louisa?" I asked.

"It was boring. It rained. You?"

"Just study," I said, watching as Mandy got up and left the shack without saying so much as good-bye. Louisa lit another cigarette. She said she loved smoking—she was like pure gagging for nicotine—but she didn't look as if she loved it. Every time she inhaled she winced. And she held the cigarette like a robot might hold one: stiffly, as if there were rules about where your fingers should be and the rate at which they should connect with your mouth. I got bored, and the smoke made me feel terrible. "You want to head back?" I asked.

"I'll just have another one," she said. "See you up there."

At dinner, Louisa and Mandy sat at a different table, even though I was the only person sitting at our usual one. It's obvious when someone is deliberately not looking at you. Their necks go rigid and they don't blink, and the rest of their face looks at you by turning red. This is what Mandy and Louisa did as they ate dinner and as they walked out afterwards. It all made the cauliflower cheese congeal inside me. I waited a minute, then walked back to my room and tried to read another book from the curriculum. But I couldn't concentrate.

Jennifer Buckley, the very short girl with curly brown hair who'd cried about her cat in the first week, knocked on my door that night. She had a cabin-sized suitcase which she rolled in carefully before sliding the door shut and resting it on the floor at her feet.

"This is Mercy," she said, unzipping the case to reveal her ginger tabby. "Isn't she beautiful?"

I oohed and ahhed and stroked even though I find cats scary in the same bony, nippy way that ferrets are.

"She is beautiful," I lied. Then I told the truth: "I understand how much you need her here. I'm taking this information..." I put out my hand as if her secret were lying on it, then put it in my mouth. "And I'm eating it." I chewed and swallowed. "It's gone."

After Jennifer, no one knocked on my door to unleash their woes. Maybe they didn't need me anymore. Maybe they'd formed solid friendships now and could tell each other. Was I sad about this? Or was I glad? All I know is that my cubicle suddenly felt completely separate from the rest of the school. A whole other world.

Oh shite, an island.

Eventually, someone else did knock on my door. It was Mandy, but she didn't have a secret.

"Hey Mand!" I said.

"Hi…I have to tell you some things," she said, declining my offer to sit next to me on the bed. She was still withholding eye contact too, which is totally creepy when someone's talking to you. "First, I split up with Andrew."

"Oh no, I'm so sorry, I know…"

"It's fine," she interrupted, moving her eyes from the window to the mirror. "Second…Oh god, I'm just going to say it! John told me to tell you you're chucked." She was actually tweaking her new bangs as she spoke.

"Well, that's no surprise."

"Are you okay about it?" She looked at me, at last.

I thought for a moment. "Yes." And I was. What I wasn't okay about was Mandy. She was so rude and distant. Why wouldn't she sit down? Why did she have to stand over me, all rigid and threatening? Why were her eyes so mean?

"Have I done something to upset you?" I asked.

"No." Eyes away again. Back to the mirror. Was she happy with her legs in her new high-waisted shorts?

"I know you, Mand. I know you're angry."

"All right. I'll tell you this. It's just that you've been so dull since you came here. You do nothing but study and you're in your room like *all* the time."

"I'm working…"

"I know you are. That's all you do, apart from acting like you're some confession-taking priest." She was now touching up her lips with the lip-gloss she'd retrieved from the pocket of her shorts. "What's that all about? Everyone's saying it's like big time strange. Everyone's saying they're not gonna tell you anything anymore. Me and Louisa especially." Mwaa Mwaa. Her lips were done.

"I don't ask people to tell me stuff."

"Has anyone said anything about me?" Back at me again. Not nice eyes. Take them away. Give them back to the mirror.

"Mandy, you know I don't tell."

"Well, it's pissing me off. Secrecy pisses me off. Since coming here, I realize you've never really told me anything about your-self and I've told you everything! You never give back, you know. You just suck people in and hold your breath."

"I'm sorry."

"It's weird. You're weird." With this, she turned around, opened my door, and left without shutting it.

CHAPTER SEVEN

In the months before christmas, the only thing I did other than study was eat. It made me feel better, and I have to admit I didn't feel well. Perhaps because I'd cut my family off and because my friends seemed to have cut me off.

If anyone wanted to tell me secrets (and there were very few now) I refused to listen. "I'm sorry, I just don't want to hear," I'd say. After a while, all the girls stopped asking. Perhaps they resented that I knew too much. Perhaps they no longer needed to confess, having sorted themselves into gaggles of friends— the Populars, the Sporty types, the Keeners (i.e., geeks), the Internationals, the Emos, the Goths, the Bi's, the Brains, etc., etc. I didn't belong to any of the groups. I was alone. I ate everything on offer in the dining hall and visited Sammy in the afternoons for one of his famous curry dishes.

Mandy became entrenched in the Populars, which included Amelia and her clone, Taahnya. This group spent all their time bitching about others, doing makeovers, and swapping clothes.

Louisa flitted between Mandy and the Populars and a group of studious types from Asia (the Internationals). One morning while I was waiting in the queue for breakfast, I got chatting with one of the Internationals, Jan. She came from China, but her Scottish accent was perfect.

"You a friend of Louisa's?" she said.

"We come from the same island," I told her.

"She's good at English. Probably be dux."

Louisa. Dux. Hmm. A few months ago this would have sent me straight to the library. I still wanted to succeed, but somehow, I didn't have the energy to compete for glory.

One evening, Amelia came into my room to ask for help with a math question. "Hi, Rachel," she said. "I am going crazy with this. Have you got a moment?" This soft, kind voice was new. I hadn't heard it since she'd said good-bye to her parents on the first day. Somehow, though, it seemed completely natural. I worked through the problem with her. She said thanks sweetly afterwards, but as she slid the door shut to enter the hallway (i.e., the real world) this flash of humanity flew to the wind because Jennifer Buckley accidentally bumped into her ("Out of my way, turd!"). Somehow, I didn't mind too much. I knew we both had our own pressures and our own ways of coping.

With no friends at Aberfeldy Halls, Sammy became my best pal. With him, I felt kind of light, like a single slice of fluffy white bread. He made no assumptions about me. He had no expectations. He called me R. I called him S.

Having decided I was more bottled up than ketchup, he devised silly games to try and un-bottle me. "There are four essential ingredients for happiness," he said. "Fresh air...exercise...and giggling."

"That's three," I said.

"Aha...the fourth is the most important one. You have to work that one out for yourself."

I had no interest in working it out. But I enjoyed the first three. All his games involved these components. Our three-legged race, for instance, went like this:

1. In the park behind the shops, S ties his foot to mine. It's windy. We've never stood so close before.

2. S puts his arm around my waist. I worry that he might notice I've been eating too much.

3. I put my arm around his. Three parts of my body are in direct contact with his. These parts feel tingly.

4. S says, "Let's walk first, then run when I say."

5. We walk slowly, our strides matching after six or seven

steps, then he says, "Run!" and we run towards the pond, and all the way around it. We are a good team. We go faster and faster.

6. S says, "Stop!" but I don't do it fast enough and when he stops and I don't, I trip and drag him to the ground with me. We giggle. It's been a long time since I've giggled. My jaw hurts with it. I don't want him to untie our feet.

We met most afternoons for several weeks after that, never talking about secrets or study or feelings or family, just playing silly games. One Friday, I'd taken the bus into town with the rest of the girls. This was the big weekly event for our school. It had been fun the first time—Louisa, Mandy, and I had eaten McDonald's and tried on makeup. But after the second time (when Mandy decided to steal a jumper from Asda with Taahnya—not even nice a jumper—and Louisa had asked me to go buy cigarettes from the newsagents 'cause I looked older than her), it stressed and bored me in equal measures. This particular time, Jan the International asked if she could window shop with me. god bless Jan, but she was more boring than fencing, so I told her I had to meet someone and hopped on the local bus back to Balbir's.

S and I strolled along the river for an hour, sat on the bank, and played "tickle-o." This involved taking turns to tickle each other's nostrils with a blade of grass. The first to give in and laugh was the loser. Sammy's record was one minute. Mine was forty seconds. I was determined to beat him this time. My eyes were watering as he sat opposite me, cross-legged, and carefully tantalized my left nasal passage with his blade. As usual, he tried to catch me unawares mid-game...

"So...why didn't you go home for the October holidays?" he asked.

"I wanted to study," I said, glad of the distraction. If I didn't scratch my nose soon I would explode.

"So..." he said, switching to the right nostril, "what made your parents leave the city?"

"I don't know. I was nine." S had managed to get the blade three centimeters up. The stopwatch on his phone had reached 47 seconds. Fourteen to go. But it felt like he was tickling my gray matter. Pain-tears were falling from my eyes. I yelled, flicked his hand away, fell back on the grass, and rubbed my nose with my hand while laughing uncontrollably. Why hadn't anyone ever told me how wonderful silliness is?

He was dumb as dog poo. No, that's rude. He just wasn't academic. Never read books or watched the news. Hated math and science. Wanted to take over the curry shop. End of story. It was much more fun, and much simpler, than it had ever been with Mandy, but it was similar in that we were perfectly incompatible and therefore the best of pals.

• • •

Speaking of Mandy. I'd never thought of her as the bullying type. I'd never thought of me as the victim type. But a few things happened in December that put us both in those unfamiliar categories.

The first was the school dance. Girls would be bussed into town to meet boys who'd also be bussed into town. I hadn't planned on going, but the dance just happened to be on the same date as my seventeenth birthday. My mother and my father showed up that afternoon to take me out for a treat. They'd visited a few times beforehand, most notably during the October break, when they took me to a chick flick in Perth (my father fell asleep) and then to an Italian restaurant in Crieff (my mother's forced smile ruined my appetite). I wasn't ever mean to them, but I refused to let them get to me, as if I'd wrapped layers of insulation around me. Not reading letters and not taking every single call (my mother called every second night) was part of this self-preservation.

As we left for my birthday treat, I noticed that they

seemed to be walking on eggshells with me, like different people altogether.

"You seem very tired, Rachel. Are you okay?" my mother said.

"They're feeding you well!" my father said when he put his arm around me.

We had Devonshire tea in some farm shop in the middle of nowhere. It was yummy, and afterwards my mother handed me a present—a dress—accompanied by an affectionate (out-of-character) plea to "have some fun, my darling, you need to have fun!" The dress was from Quiz. It was sparkly and way shorter than anything I'd ever been allowed to wear before. I approved. I kissed her and my father. And I went to the dance.

It freaked me out. Reminded me of the dreaded island dances, with girls waiting for boys to ask them to dance, kiss, and more. One boy from Baltyre asked me to dance, which I did. Then he asked me again, which I did. And again. Did. It was boring. His name was Bill. When we twirled it stifled and dizzied me. He was reasonably tall and good looking, I suppose, but he had breath so hot it could steam cooked cauliflower. And he kept breathing into my ear as he tried to converse (So, *Rachel*, where did you learn to dance? So, *Rachel*, we should meet up in town…). By the end of the fourth dance, his breath had turned to precipitation and was dripping down from my ear.

His hands were on my buttocks. I moved out to do a twirl to dislodge them then told him I needed to go to the bathroom. As disgusting as I found Bill, I was glad to have had him to dance with, because the girls all seemed to be avoiding me and the thought of approaching them made me hyperventilate. Nothing in the world—not roller coasters or blinking statues or *The Sixth Sense*—is as scary as a group of girls who've decided you're a dickhead. Thankfully, when I came out of the bathroom, the bus had arrived to take us home. Couples crammed a final snog before boarding.

On the bus on the way home, Mandy sat in the back with Aimee. For a while, they giggled about the boys they'd danced with (Peter, who had very sweaty hands; Jamie, who pressed up against Aimee and definitely had a boner; Brian, who had dandruff all over his black shirt; Paul, who was just too gorgeous and at the end had put his hand down psss psss psss—Aimee whispered the rest of that bit—and she shouldn't say this but she *really* liked it.). As the bus neared the school, the chat decreased in volume, but I could hear Mandy saying to Aimee: "She's a tease…dances with poor Bill all night, then just says good-bye, leaves him dangling."

"That's so not fair," Aimee said.

"Totally. Typical," Mandy said.

Then, while I was trying to get to sleep, I realized Mandy and Taahnya were with Amelia O'Donohue and had chosen her cubicle—i.e., the one right next to mine—to backstab me big time. Her many comments included:

Teases the boys. So like cruel.

Screwed up.

Scandal!

Off-the-wall unhappy family. The whole island thinks so.

"Guys, stop being f…ing bitches," Amelia interrupted. "You know she can hear. Plus, it's boring. I'm going to watch *CSI*."

Amelia's display of integrity surprised me, but it didn't stop Mandy and Taahnya from continuing after she left for the telly room…

Completely unable to have fun.

Sent away…

Boring…

Looked daft in that dress. Did you see how short it was? From Quiz! Like the one I got two years ago.

Never tells anyone anything.

Studies like all the time.

Has no friends.

"I can hear you!" I said loudly. "Perhaps you'd like to chat about me elsewhere?"

Silence for a moment, then giggling, then they moved their conversation to another room down the hall, where I could still hear them.

It felt truly awful. I'd never been so betrayed in my life. No one else knew it was my birthday, but Mandy did. How could she be so mean? I cried for ages.

The following evening, just after Miss Rose announced that supper was ready, the loudspeaker crackled, a door banged over the speaker, someone tapped loudly on the microphone, then Mandy's voice pounded through the dorms, clear as day, and said: "Rachel Ross is a Keener!"

I tried not to cry as I made my way over to the dining hall. Mandy and Amelia and Louisa sat at the table near the window. I sat with Jan and the International girls who chatted away in Cantonese (I think). I ate. No talking. Then went to my bed to cry.

• • •

The incidents continued right up until christmas. They froze into my bones along with the weather: a wet black winter that weighed on my forehead like two bricks, then three, and so on. Hours of sunlight: none. There was backstabbing, loud-speaker announcements, and, once, I got into bed to find Coco Pops all over my sheets. I'd tried to ignore the bullying till then, but it was now making me feel so hard and sore inside that I wanted to explode. I found myself walking as fast as I could, thinking, "Ignore them, ignore them," and when I finally stopped walking I realized I was at the curry shop. S saw me and came out.

"Hey! What's wrong? You look upset."

"Nothing," I said, panting from the angry power walk.

He lifted his hand to my hair and I felt the skin on my neck go bumpy. Was he going to hug me? Kiss me?

"What's this?" he asked, holding a small brown thing in his hand and examining it.

"A Coco Pop." I sighed and shook my head.

Before I could say, "Don't ask!" he'd raced into the shop and reemerged with a bowl and some milk.

"Ha ha," I said, more relaxed already.

Sammy kept me sane. He didn't have a clue about what was going on at school, and treated me like a normal everyday person. By the end of December I'd gotten sick of his curries, but our friendship, or something anyway, made me feel fresh, happy, and optimistic.

• • •

"This is for you," he said, the day before I had to leave for the christmas break.

I opened the beautifully wrapped present. Inside was a bottle of ketchup.

"That's stupid," I said.

He was like, "Rachel, I know we're only young, and I know you told me like *nothing* about yourself, but…"

"Don't say any more."

"I really like you…In fact…"

"Shhh."

"Take the present home. Open it. There's something inside."

• • •

I got a bus the next day. Mandy and Louisa sat next to each other and talked about me the whole way. I played cool, refusing to let them see that I was upset. Anyway, I had to concentrate on getting through two weeks of the good lord.

I sat in the damp, depressing corridor-lounge of the ferry and watched the horizontal rain pelt along the windows, the hazy miserableness of the island just visible in the distance. It gave me an instant feeling of depression. When we docked, and I walked out along the ramp, my mother and my father were waiting for me with flowers.

"Welcome home!" they said. They'd never given me flowers before and to be honest I didn't mind that. Watching living things wilt and die is not my cup of tea.

Mandy and Louisa's parents were there too. They'd been chatting with my folks before we got off.

"We were just suggesting you and the girls have a sleepover?" my mother said. "I could make cupcakes."

The silence wasn't long—probably not long enough for my ignoramus parents to realize that the girls would rather eat each other's eyeballs than sleep at my house and have the stupid cupcakes I'd said I loved when I was like *four*—but it was long enough for my heartbeat to flit and flip at the speed of light.

"That sounds wonderful, doesn't it, Mandy?" her mother said.

"Yeah. We'll text you." She looked at Louisa.

Sure they would.

• • •

When we got home, a new fence had been erected along the field between our house and Mandy's house.

"What's that?" I asked.

"Oh, the Grogan's always wanted that paddock," my mother said. "We didn't use it really."

So that was how they could afford my school fees. They'd sold half our land to Mandy's family. The realization made me gulp loudly. Swallow the guilt. There, it's gone.

That night, my parents took me out to dinner in the only

posh restaurant on the island—we'd been once when I was tiny, during a holiday before we moved from Edinburgh. I remember we sang funny songs and played I-Spy for the five hours it took to get there. To my surprise, my mother and my father didn't say grace, and I'm sure I saw them holding hands under the table when I came back from the loo. Strange. They hadn't shown any signs of affection for years.

That night, my mother came to my room to say good night. As soon as I heard the door opening, I pounced to the floor to say my prayers.

"…thank you for everything and sorry for my sins and please may I have some humility to the power of infinity. Amen."

I stood up and got into bed. My mother tucked me in and kissed my forehead and said, "I love you, Rachel. It's so good to have you home."

The next morning over salty porridge, my father found something other than evil politicians in *The Scotsman*. "Look at this, will you, Claire?" he said, using my mother's actual name.

"Mmm," she said, reading from the Jobs section. All I saw was the heading: "Broadcast Journalist."

"That looks perfect." She patted him on the shoulder and put on the kind of real coffee we used to have in happier times in Edinburgh. I remember my father used to get up before us and put it on every morning. "Ah," my mother would say back then, waking beside me (I always ended up in bed with them in those days). Inhaling the coffee fumes, she'd carry me from the bedroom to the kitchen and squash me between them as she kissed my father full on the lips.

This slip back to our olden days was very odd indeed, but not as odd as christmas.

• • •

christmas was Sunday, and we started by going to church, just as we always did on Sundays, holding umbrellas, wearing thick coats, heads and shoulders down towards the ground where our lives also were.

We listened to the chant-like hymns, the sermon filled with doom and gloom and not-happy occasions.

The strange thing was that everyone looked at us oddly, like we were freaks, and while I would have agreed that my parents were in that category, I wasn't, and it felt awful.

John was in the back row, just behind the Grogans. I turned around during the service and nodded at him. His mother elbowed him in the side. He winced, then looked at the floor.

Outside afterwards, Mandy and Louisa were chatting with him. They watched me come out of the church, giving me spectacularly dirty looks.

Even Mrs. Crookston from the corner shop managed a one-eyed dirty look. For some reason, our family was being ostracized.

"I've quit the paper," my father said as we walked home.

"Why?"

"Because it was contributing to my slow and painful demise."

What?

As we walked home, I spotted Bronte, the girl I'd met in hospital before going to Aberfeldy Halls. She was pushing a stroller along the main street.

"Hi Bronte," I said, trying to catch her eyes, which were lurking underneath the hood of her huge padded coat.

She looked up, startled, then said hello nervously, before returning her eyes to their previous position and walking on with her wailing baby.

When we got home, my father did something outrageous. He said, "Damn it, Claire, let's go for a drive and a walk and let's put the radio on full blast."

On a Sunday!

We drove to the other end of the island and parked the car on the side of the road. "We're going on an adventure. To the cave of the winds," my father said. For two miles, we trekked along the beach. My mother and my father held hands most of the way, except when we stopped to skim stones (I won.

Five skips on the bumpy black water) and compete in a long jump competition (My mother won. She used to be a champ at it back when, apparently). There was an uncanny amount of giggling going on. Maybe they'd been *doing it* while I was away, I thought, before thinking, don't think about that for god's sake, stop, oh gross, I'm seeing them, No!

The cave of the winds was just a small dark cave, not even big enough to stand up in. None of us knew why they called it that and going inside didn't enlighten us. There was no wind, just a few empty cans of Foster's.

I'd never known them to be such cheery rebels. It was weird as all hell. And while it was weird as all hell in a good way, I still counted the minutes before I could leave again.

That night, my mother caught me emptying tomato ketchup into the bathroom sink.

"What are you doing?" she asked.

"Oh, just…I need the bottle for an experiment," I lied.

She accepted this lame excuse and left me alone to discover a ball of tinfoil. Inside, was a note: *Woods. Sunday before first day of term. 7:00 p.m. We need to kiss.*

• • •

The week after christmas was quiet and uneventful. I studied, mostly, and got drawn into two endless games of Monopoly.

My parents had taken to experimental cooking with the radio on (Current music! Loud! Cooking together!). We'd marked the new recipes out of ten before an evening walk and a movie (When did they get satellite?). The night before Hogmanay, my mother came into my room. "I need to talk to you about the dance tomorrow," she said.

"Don't worry, I'm not going."

"Are you sure?"

"I am."

"I think you're right," she said.

• • •

Mandy and Louisa continued to ignore me on the long journey back to school. I felt flat and exhausted by the time we arrived. The island had sapped my energy and all I wanted to do was sleep.

But I couldn't. I had to see Sammy. I'd thought about nothing else. And when 7:00 p.m. came, I dragged myself from my bed and walked down into the woods.

I followed the dirt track from the back of the dorms all the way to the small derelict shack at the other end. Sammy hadn't told me to go there, but it was *the* meeting place, and I assumed that's where he'd be. I opened the wobbly wooden door expecting to find him, and gasped when I saw the girl with the ponytail kissing Mr. Burns, the PE teacher.

My gasp was a quiet one, so they didn't notice as I walked backwards out of the shack, and shut the door carefully behind me. Blimey, a teacher kissing a student. Imagine the trouble he'd be in if anyone found out.

"Boo!" Sammy jumped out from behind a tree.

"Shh," I said grabbing his hand and running back up the track.

We stopped in a clearing in the middle of the woods.

"What's wrong?" he asked.

I was like, "Nothing, that place spooks me."

"I missed you," he said, kissing me. I'm not sure if I kissed him back. But I liked it. I liked him. He tasted even more delicious than the food he made. He felt even more cozy than my favorite red duvet cover. Nothing like John, who tasted like Irn-Bru and whose tongue felt like sandpaper. It scared me to death, how nice it felt.

"I have to go back to the dorms," I said. "I'll get in trouble."

"Can I see you tomorrow?"

"Maybe…" I raced off as fast as my body would take me, then lay in my bed and thought about the kiss. The warm, perfect kiss.

Oh dear, this wasn't supposed to happen. This thing with Sammy had gone too far. This would unravel me, unravel everything.

I wouldn't let it. I would put Sammy away somewhere safe and un-gettable.

So I didn't meet Sammy the following afternoon. I avoided the curry shop from then on.

CHAPTER EIGHT

I can't remember exactly when the girls got fed up with tormenting me. Not long after christmas, I think, they began to realize that my lack of response gave them no pleasure. Also, Louisa started to realize that I was the only person she could be outwardly clever with. She came to my room a few times on the sly to talk over math problems. To add to that, Mandy and Taahnya et al., had discovered that Jan, the International girl, cried when they called her a chinky. Before long, she was the one whose bed was filled with Coco Pops. Poor Jan.

Something had changed in me around christmas time, anyway. I felt energetic, invigorated, and focused. I no longer cared about whether Mandy and Louisa liked me. I'd stopped taking the buses into town on Fridays. Girls giggling with stupid boys. Girls buying makeup and tops. Girls shoplifting and telling everyone. Fridays in town were not for me. It did my nut in. I had no interest in anything but work. And work I did. I read all the books on the English reading list three times, then found all the literary criticism I could in the library, then wrote two practice essays for each. I liked my one on T. S. Eliot's "The Love Song of J. Alfred Prufrock" the best. But my take on John Irving's *A Prayer for Owen Meany* was pretty original, if I do say so myself. I managed to get all the exam papers for the past three years in biology, math, physics, and chemistry, and had them down pat after four or five attempts. In between, I handed in all my assignments and essays with pride and confidence. I was pretty good at this academic malarkey.

I don't know how Louisa managed to stay in with the Populars and work so hard, but she did. Maybe it was just the smoking. An inordinate amount of cool bonding seemed to take place on the fire escapes. Louisa studied almost as much as I did, and always got As. She and I were constantly looking at each other as papers were handed back, wondering who'd done better. It was always very close.

• • •

Through January, February, and March, the only incident that varied my study routine happened on the night of the second school dance. I stayed behind this time, with girls who felt too ugly or too hip or too devoted to boyfriends from elsewhere to go. Surprisingly, Amelia O'Donohue was one of them. "The boys are idiots and the girls are worse," I overheard her saying to Taahnya. "I'd rather watch the telly." Which is what she did. Nonstop.

I was writing an English essay at my desk when my door opened and closed and Sammy stood before me, just like that.

"How did you get in here?"

"Just walked in the front entrance. What's wrong with you?"

"Nothing."

"We have the most perfect moment then you disappear for months."

"I'm sorry, but I'm not interested in getting involved."

"I've never met anyone like you, Rachel Ross. You're infuriating. You're the cleverest person I've ever met and you're funny and incredibly easy to be around, but it's like you've tuned everything out. How can you do that?"

"I'm just motivated."

"No. I don't think it's that. You're scared."

"I am not."

"Then kiss me. And I don't mean let me kiss you. I mean kiss *me*."

"No."

"Why not?"

"You may not understand this, but I have one goal. I don't want anything to screw it up."

Before I had time to stop him, Sammy grabbed me old-movie style and kissed me violently. I didn't succumb or soften, I pushed him away and yelled, "Get out of here! How dare you? I never want to see you again for as long as I live."

He sighed, shook his head, and walked out of my room.

• • •

By the time April came, I had taken to rearranging things in my cubicle, repeatedly cleaning out my cupboards, taking an unusual amount of pleasure from the comfort of my cocoon. Sammy left me alone, just as I'd asked. But just before the easter holidays, I bumped into him in front of the chemist.

"Hello," I said.

"That all you're going to say?"

"Aye."

"You know what? You're screwed up. There's something wrong with you. I give up," he said.

"Good." I headed along the road and up the driveway.

But he didn't give up. He ran after me. "You make me angry," he said. "I don't usually do angry."

"Sammy, I'm sorry. I didn't mean to hurt you. I'm just not interested in getting into anything. I want to be a doctor. I want to go to Oxford."

"Well, I'm not going to stop you. A kiss won't stop you."

"Can you just leave me alone?"

"Right, fine," he said. "I'll leave you alone. Like everyone else leaves you alone. So you can study alone. Work alone. Die alone…"

"Shut up," I said, upping my pace and leaving him dangling at the end of the driveway.

• • •

I didn't go home for easter. I read, revised, took notes, went over practice exams, worked, worked, worked. I hardly spoke to a soul. I told my mother and my father that all communication was on hold until after my exams. Reluctantly, they agreed.

Word had spread that the probable dux of the school would be asked to do a motivational speech before the higher exams began. I knew, and everyone knew, that it was between me and Louisa MacDonald. When the principal, a business-like man called Mr. Gillies, called me to the office, I guessed what it was about.

"You are an inspiration," he said, as I sat opposite his desk. Mr. Gillies always wore blue suits and brown shoes. He said short sharp hellos to everyone as he strode purposefully through the school (hello.hello.hello). I'd never heard him say anything else before now. "Every teacher has nothing but praise for you," he said. "Your practice exam results were the best this school has ever achieved. Would you do a speech at assembly before the first exam? To motivate the girls?"

"Of course," I said, feeling ambivalent about it. All the girls hated me. I was a hermit, a Keener, a Brain. An ambitious, dour-faced, boring, friendless, loveless Brain. How could I motivate them?

As I walked out of his office, Louisa spotted me from the driveway. Her eyes narrowed. She didn't like me being favored by the principal. She cared about these things more than I did.

But I have to admit, the request invigorated me. I had the most promise. I was an inspiration! Anticipation, nerves, excitement, and angry determination welled and swelled inside me as I wrote the speech ten minutes later. I was about to succeed.

I was about to escape.

CHAPTER
NINE

I ignored the wheezing for two days running, mostly because my exams were about to begin and it couldn't be! It couldn't be that my crap lungs would screw me over when I needed them most. But after two days of breathlessness, of being unable to sleep at night, I knew it wasn't going to go away and that I needed some medical help.

Nurse Craig came to school each morning and afternoon, to see a long line of girls with ailments either serious enough or not serious enough to be allowed to stay off school for the day. Her room was on the first floor (Left). I walked down the stairs in my pajamas at 7:30 a.m. The girl who'd confessed to having lupus in first semester smiled at me in the queue, as did the girl with the hairy toothy parasitic armpit twin.

"Blow into this," Nurse Craig said when it was finally my turn. I blew into the cardboard tube. "Again," she said, and I blew again, as hard as I could, which was pathetically not-hard.

"Any other symptoms?" she said.

I told her my usual symptoms had arrived—flu-like fever, sore everything. She put me on the nebulizer, gave me some aspirin, told me to rest all day, and to come back in the afternoon to see how I was getting on.

Mortified, I returned to my room. I needed to read over my English notes. I needed to make sure my grades were even higher than they'd been for my practice exams. I had no time for rest.

I'd never spent a weekday in the dorms. It was freaky. Quiet. But with noises I didn't recognize. Washing machines buzzing. Doors creaking in the distance. No voices, just erratic sounds that kept me from reading over my notes and kept me from sleeping. I lay in bed, the steroids from the nebulizer working my lungs, the aspirin working the pain in my head and everywhere else, and tried to get to sleep. Before I knew it I was having the obligatory exam dream.

I'm walking across the walkway, past the dining hall, up two flights of stairs, into the English classroom. Exam papers rest on desks before tired-looking pupils. I walk towards my desk and look at my blank answer sheet. To my horror, I realize everyone has finished. Their papers are all completed. I'm late. I've missed English.

I walk towards the window, open it, look out over the driveway, lean forward as if trying to grab something, then fall.

As I fall, I think to myself, You're not supposed to land in a dream. You're supposed to wake up mid-fall. You're supposed to sit upright in your bed, sweating, thanking god that it was just a dream.

I don't. I fall fast, all the way to the garden bed at the bottom. Bang. I land. Face down, stomach down, and it hurts, like hell.

I don't even wake up at that point. I lie face down in the garden, in agony.

Still dreaming, I roll onto my back and I look up at the school and the windows are filled with heads, all looking down at me, perplexed. The pupils are dressed in their Aberfeldy Halls uniforms, holding their completed exam papers. And look—John's there, with an enormous love-bite on his neck. Sammy's there too, looking worried. Bronte and her baby are there. My mother and my father are there, looking down at me—not dressed in school uniforms, not holding exam papers, but holding their bibles in their hands.

• • •

It was then that I woke up. Sat up. Sweating, as you should after a dream like that.

Feeling confused and disorientated, I eventually found my way, slowly, painfully, to the bathroom, and stood under the shower, dizzy and breathless. I scraped air into my lungs the way I always did at home, then fainted.

105

When I woke, the shower had gone cold and a crop of goose bumps had come to graze on my body. I stood, turned the shower off, wrapped a towel around me, walked back to my cubicle, changed my sheets, took a second dose of ventolin, seretide, and aspirin, and got back into bed. It was only 12:15 p.m. I would see the nurse at 4:00.

I picked up my revision notes for English. *Macbeth* and Keats and T. S. Eliot whizzed around the page. Nonsensical. A blur.

I needed to sleep.

But I couldn't. The day noises of the dorms had multiplied into a whir of buzzing washing machines, creaking doors, ticking clocks, and screeching cats. I put scrunched up tissues in my ears to stop the noises and dozed off for a while. When I woke, it was only fifteen minutes later, and the tissue had fallen from my right ear and the washing machine buzz and door creak had stopped but the ticking had gotten louder and so had the cat. An ugly meow. Make it stop!

My breathing was a little better. If I concentrated and tried to relax, I could take shallow breaths and feel the oxygen calm me. On the desk beside my bed, my revision notes sat neatly, ready for one last blast before my first exam, which, unsurprisingly, was English—straight after assembly tomorrow.

I lay down again and put more scrunched up tissue in my

ears. I closed my eyes. All noises but one had disappeared into a light muffled hum, the background for a cat that was so loud it must surely be in the building.

Had to be Jennifer Buckley's, I thought to myself. I don't know how she'd managed to keep the poor red mite quiet since September, but I'd never heard him meow, and no one had ever mentioned her stowaway secret.

What floor was Jennifer on? I wondered, sitting up, unable to sleep, desperate to placate the cat in order to get some rest and recover in time for my first exam. I wasn't sure, so I put my dressing gown on and followed the noise down the corridor. It was the loudest cat I'd ever heard. The loudest and the creepiest. Its meow sent prickles of anxiety up my legs and through my body. It stopped my breathing. It stopped my whole body, smack bang in the middle of my floor, the third floor, the bathroom door in front of me, the vast linen cupboards beside. I blocked my ears to stop the noise that was piercing into me, then opened the linen cupboard door.

It was dark inside. The hall light took awhile to make its way inside and when it did I couldn't find the cat. Only sheets and pillowcases and towels. White fluffy towels. All at the back of the cupboard. Thank god, the noise had stopped. I was about to shut the cupboard door and walk away. But one of the towels moved. The cat must be underneath, I thought, reaching towards the wriggling lump with trembling fingers.

I lifted the moving towel and held it in my hand, trying to see what had been stirring underneath it. I moved my head closer, my pointless asthmatic breaths the soundtrack for the horror that was about to begin.

Because inside the cupboard, underneath the towel I'd retrieved, wriggling red in its manchester bed, was a baby. A tiny newborn baby boy, its cord freshly cut, its smooth skin covered in warm womb gunk, its dark eyes shining a single bright light into mine, a laser beam so sharp it shot me backwards and onto the ground.

CHAPTER
TEN

f I tell, I'll go to hell.

The words echoed in my head as I lay on the hall floor, unable to breathe. What first? *The Thing* in the cupboard? Had there really been a baby, lying there, gurgling, its cry answered at last, by someone, but not by the right someone? Or had I imagined it the way I sometimes imagined living in a high-rise flat overlooking lights-lights-lights of city-not-island? Had I been devoid of air too long? My lungs squeezing what it could from around it—images, sounds—if not air? And had these messages bottle-necked their way to my brain to make me see *The Thing*, this red gooey creature that did not really exist?

I needed to stand up, look again, and be sure. But I couldn't, not without ventolin. Rasping, I made it onto my knees and crawled at snail speed along the hall, counting the twenty doors as I passed, eager to make it to number nineteen. Finally, sliding my cubicle door open from ground level, I saw the blue beacon of life on my desk. The very image gave me the strength to stand.

Oh, sweet ventolin, opening my throat a little, enough for me to contemplate what needed to be done next.

I looked out the windows across to the dining hall. The boarders were queuing for their lunch, talking noisily, unaware. I peeked into the hall I'd crawled along. As before, there was no one there. I counted: *in-two-three, out-two-three* and then walked towards the bathroom, hoping I'd hallucinated, but when I reached the cupboard, opened it, and shone my flashlight towards the back, a now-sleeping baby winced its closed eyes at my light.

I had no experience with babies. I had no idea what to do with it, its face scrunched, its tiny bluish fingers gnarled into fists. I touched the top of its head, soft and squidgy like play dough. Who in this huge old building had secretly given birth? Who was so frightened that they had simply hidden the thing and gone on as if nothing had happened?

I thought hard about what to do. Call Miss Rose? Call the police? An ambulance? What would be the repercussions for the mother? What would she want me to do? What would she be feeling?

When people told me their problems, many of them painful and disgusting and sad, my strategy was to empathize, to try and imagine how I would feel if that secret was mine. When I considered what to do about the baby and its mother, I found myself thinking about this strategy and recalling one incident in particular. Before now, this had been my biggest secret.

· · ·

I was nine. We lived in Edinburgh. My parents had been having a rocky time for several months. My father had been promoted and was always away. My mother was lonely. She and my father argued over the phone all the time.

"All I wanted was you and Rach and another baby, and you've abandoned me here. And now we've left it too late!" my mother had said.

I recalled she made a new friend at work, which cheered her up a bit. He was shorter than she was, with a tiny nose and unruly ginger hair. He made me feel a bit queasy ("What a big girl you are!" he'd say every single time he saw me). Not that I have anything against gingers.

I recalled finding her and her new friend in the bathtub when I was supposed to be sleeping in bed. His bum was up in the air. It had lines of wet dark red hair on it.

"Now Rachel," my mother said as she'd tucked me in after drying herself. "I want you to promise me something."

"What?" I said.

"I want you to promise you'll never tell Daddy what you saw tonight."

"Why?"

"Because I'm asking you."

"Are you getting a divorce?"

"No."

"Are you going to run away with the little red man?"

"No."

"Do you promise you won't?"

"Do you promise not to tell?"

"Okay," I said quietly, without conviction.

"Pinky promise," she said.

We curled our pinkies around each other's. She kissed me and turned off the light.

But I didn't empathize. I didn't understand at all. I guess this might be why I didn't keep my pinky promise, why I told my father, why we ended up on the island waiting to be saved—miserable, regretful, sad.

• • •

Looking at the sleeping child, I vowed I would not make the same mistake I made when I was nine. I would keep this secret. I would help the poor girl who had hidden her pregnancy and her labor.

I gathered my thoughts. What were the facts?

1. Obviously, the mother did not want anyone to know about this.
2. She would be terrified of getting into the most massive trouble imaginable.
3. She'd be in pain.
4. She'd need help.

I wrapped the sleeping baby in a towel and carried it to my cubicle. First things first. I had to make sure it was okay and find a safe place to hide it.

The bell rang. I watched as the dining hall emptied and girls exited for their afternoon classes. I could see Amelia O'Donohue walking towards the school building. I could see the girl with the ponytail who'd kissed the gym teacher and my ex-best friends Mandy Grogan and Louisa MacDonald. I could see Miss Rose chatting with the chef.

It was still asleep on my bed. From my biology studies, I knew enough to understand that the mother had obviously taken care of the placenta and umbilical cord. I checked the baby's pulse, which seemed normal. The baby was a healthy color. Hence, there seemed to be no immediate health issues to deal with. But it would need milk soon and, most worryingly, it would eventually wake up and cry. Which meant I had to find a safe place to hide it quick.

CHAPTER
ELEVEN

I remembered the darkroom on the second floor (Right). In the months since I'd arrived, increasingly bizarre suggestions for its use had been listed on the sheet on the door (smoking room/backstabbing room/hopping room), but nothing had been decided. It hadn't been decorated or changed in any way.

I put the swaddled baby on some towels in my plastic laundry basket and carried it downstairs, praying that no one would see me en route.

"How you feeling?" Nurse Craig made me jump. She was looking up from the first floor landing. What was she doing there?

"A bit better," I said, terrified that my washing would wake up and howl. "I thought you were only here mornings and afternoons."

"I'm doing some research work on the side. My husband's not working at the moment so it's much quieter here. You don't look well at all. Come at five to four, beat the others."

"I will. Thanks."

"And get back to bed."

"Okay," I said, not getting back to bed, but walking with my hamper onto the second floor.

Someone else must have been off sick on the second floor. The television was on. I tiptoed to the old darkroom. It was the same size as my cubicle, but with sturdy, reasonably sound-proof, full-height walls. Thankfully, the key was still in the door. I unlocked the door, relieved to find it as abandoned as it had been at the beginning of the school year. Inside was a trestle table with photographic paper, trays, chemicals, staplers, and other stationery. At the other end of the room, was a hefty built-in cupboard. Locking the door behind me, I placed the hamper on the floor, looked inside to check that the baby was still sleeping and thought for a moment.

I opened the built-in cupboard at the end of the room. Taking several towels from the hamper, I made a soft bed, placed the wrapped baby on top, and closed the cupboard door, careful to leave a crack for air. I then stepped outside the darkroom, locked the door, and hid the key in my dressing gown pocket.

• • •

I'm clever. I have to admit.

Nurse Craig answered the door as soon as I knocked.

"I know I'm early. But I'm out of ventolin," I said. "Please can I go to the chemist before the crowds descend?"

"Are you sure you're well enough to walk?"

"I am. The fresh air might do me good."

I changed into my tracksuit then wrote on a large piece of paper: NEWSFLASH: *If I Tell Clinic Now Open.* TONIGHT, ALO. *Rachel Ross's cubicle, Third Floor (Right).*

It was worth a try, I thought, as I walked down to the ground floor and pinned the notice on the board.

The chemist was next to the curry shop. I was wheezing like mad by the time I made it there. I had terrible trouble walking, but eventually I found myself inside the bright, crammed store.

"Hi," I said, placing nappies, wipes, a baby monitor, long-life ready-mixed formula milk, and a bottle on the counter. Before the fifty-something assistant could look at me strangely, I added. "My aunty had a boy! She's bringing him to show me after school."

She was like, "Ah, what's his name?"

"Sorry?"

"The baby. He *does* have a name…"

I went blank. I couldn't think of a single name. Not one. After a while, the word Rachel went through my head, but that was my name.

"Are you all right?" The woman asked.

"Asthma. Sorry," I said. "Can I get a ventolin? Nurse Craig said she'd ring ahead."

"Ah yes, she did. Just a moment."

By the time the bagged ventolin made its way to the counter, I'd thought of a name.

"It's Sam," I said.

"Oh, that's lovely. Sam boy or Sam girl?"

"Sam boy."

"That's £34.56," she said, putting the baby stuff in the bag.

I handed her the £50 my parents had given me for treats etc., asked for a second bag so no one could see what was inside, tied it securely, and left as fast as I could.

"Oy!" someone yelled.

Bugger, it was Sammy.

"Are you okay? Why are you off school?"

"I'm fine. I can't talk now," I said.

But he was like, "You're sick! Can I help you?"

"I'm fine!" I snapped, not looking back.

I am clever, I thought, as I headed back to school with the

strangest bag of shopping ever. If I hadn't fainted before I made it to the dorms, I'd have continued to think I was the cleverest person in the entire universe.

CHAPTER
TWELVE

When I woke up I was in the sick room.

"Rachel! Rachel!" Miss Rose's face was an inch from my nebulizer. I shrieked when I saw her, took the mask off, sat bolt upright and nearly head-butted her.

"Where's my shopping?"

"I put it in your room," Miss Craig said. "We're going to take you to the hospital, Rachel."

"No, no, no!" I said, probably too insistent, looking back. "I'm fine. I really feel fine. I just shouldn't have walked to the shop."

What if they took me to hospital? What would I do then? What would happen to the baby? Its mother?

"Honestly," I said, putting on a calm, I-can-breathe, voice. "I think I just need some sleep."

They looked at me for a few moments as I tried hard to make my breathing sound normal. With each tiny gulp of air, I *sensed* the baby. It wasn't that I saw it in my mind, or that I smelled or felt or heard it. It was all my senses prickling together, asking: *Is it all right? Am I mad keeping this a secret? Am I doing the right thing? Please let it be safe.*

Miss Rose's voice whooshed me back into the real, non-baby world, "Are you sure you're okay?"

"Absolutely. I'm going to be fine by morning. I'm going to do the speech and my English exam."

"Don't worry about that now."

"I'm not. I'm not. But I will."

"If you're well enough."

"I will be well enough."

"All right then. But I want to ring your mother, just to let her know. She's been leaving messages for you, Rachel. You should call her back."

My mother and my father were the last people I wanted to talk to. Hadn't they gotten the hint? I just couldn't let them distract me, judge me, or get me down. Too much was at stake.

"Nurse, you take Rachel to her cubicle," Miss Rose said.

I started to feel angry after Nurse Craig finally left my cubicle. The last thing I needed was pressure from my parents, as well as someone else's (massive) (incredible) (baby-shaped) problem. I looked at the speech I'd written for the pre-exam assembly. I was pleased with it. It went like this:

Girls of Aberfeldy Halls, it is my privilege to stand among you on the eve of our adult lives. The following weeks will determine our success and our happiness. And we should ask ourselves: Are we proud? Have we done everything we can to achieve our goals?

It's because of this fine school that I'm sure each one of us can answer:

Yes, I am.

And: Yes, I have.

Good luck, girls.

I put the speech down, glanced at my English notes, and smashed my fist on my desk in rage. How was I ever going to make the speech and excel in my higher exams? This could ruin everything. My chances of getting into uni. My chances of leaving the island that had straight-jacketed my life-so-far.

I waited about half an hour and then warmed a bottle of milk using a saucepan of hot water from the communal kitchen. The dorms were still eerily empty and quiet. The television had been switched off. As I approached the darkroom, I could hear it. A faint cat noise, like the one I'd first heard.

It was awake.

I locked the door from the inside and picked the baby up,

holding it in my arms as it guzzled three quarters of the bottle. I put a nappy on it, wrapped it in a sheet, and plugged in the baby monitor. Once it was settled, I went back to my cubicle, turned on the receiving end of the baby monitor so that a light came on if it made a noise, and began my investigations.

My very own *Who-Had-It.*

CHAPTER THIRTEEN

Amelia O'Donohue is *so* not a virgin.

It could be her, I thought as I sat at my desk making notes. I'd been on watch for her secret rendezvous at least twice a week during the first few months at Aberfeldy Halls.

Her boyfriend, whose name turned out to be Piers—a suitably posh name for a posh chinless dick—would arrive ALO and text her (illegal) mobile to indicate that he was on the fire escape. A few seconds later, she'd pop her head over the top of the cubicle wall and look down at me while I said the words: *If I tell, I'll go to hell.*

She couldn't even be bothered coming into my cubicle after the first couple of times, so I'd have to stand on my bed for the cheek-slap and nose-pull.

I'd listen as she sprayed perfume, changed clothes, and then I'd do everything in my power to stop people from going out on the fire escape or entering her room.

After a while, she stopped asking me to guard her room. She

felt confident, I suppose, as no one had tried to find her after the first few times I stopped them.

I'd snuck peeks several times and knew they'd been going all the way for some time now.

And she'd put on weight. "It's the stodge they feed us," she'd say. "I'm on a carrot diet! Anyways, shut up, like, who are you to talk? You're hardly catwalk material yourself."

Come to think of it, I'd heard her vomit in the loos a while back. When I asked her later if she was feeling all right, she was like, "None of your business, stalker!"

Oh, and I'd heard her crying last Sunday. When I asked her what was wrong, she was like, "Piss off!"

Could be her.

Probably was her.

The bell rang. I watched the girls head back into the dorm building, taking note of anything unusual. There were pale girls, tired-looking girls, worried-looking girls. There was Amelia O'Donohue. I listened as she came into her room, turned her music on, and changed out of her uniform. I heard Taahnya knock, come in, and whisper something. Eventually, they both left. I stood on my bed to look into her room. Her bed was unmade. Her desk was a mess. Her clothes were strewn all over the floor. Unable to see any incriminating evidence, I climbed over the wall, landing on her bed harder than I'd anticipated.

In her cupboards were clothes and more clothes.

In her drawers were bags and bags of chocolate Flakes and licorice all sorts and five large bars of Cadbury's dairy milk chocolate and peanut butter and actual butter and four loaves of crusty bread, one of which had been disemboweled so it was only a crust now. There were underpants (lacy, frilly, see-through...) and a stethoscope!

In her toilet bag was an unopened, *untouched*, packet of tampons.

In her handbag were lipsticks and eyeliners.

On her desk was a diary...

Footsteps. I jumped back over the wall so fast I surprised myself, and huddled in bed, frightened...

...with Amelia O'Donohue's secret diary in my hot little hands.

CHAPTER FOURTEEN

Dear diary,

Friends:

Rachel Ross (though I wouldn't admit this to anyone but you, diary. She's a bit of a Keener, but the only trustworthy person in the whole entire school)

Mandy Grogan (dumb, but fun)

Louisa MacDonald (Brain, but funny)

Enemies:

Tanya Nairn (keep 'em close)

Sluts:

Tanya Nairn (She denies it, but I know for a fact she had an abortion last year)

Boyfriends:

Piers Watson-McInerney

Secrets:

1. See above re Tanya Nairn—Whose was it: John McDonald or William Collier?

2. I am in love with Piers Watson-McInerney.

3. I'm going to move in with him in three months time!

4. I can't write this last secret down. I haven't even told Rachel.

Amelia was calling to me. I slammed her diary shut, pulled my head out from under the duvet, and said "Yeah?"

"Tonight at 10:00?"

She hadn't asked me to watch out for ages. "Why?" I asked.

She opened my door. I hid her diary under the sheets just in time.

"God, you look bloody awful," she said.

"You're always really mean, Amelia. Why should I?" I wouldn't usually question her like this. But in her diary she said I was her friend. If so, why did she treat me like dog crap?

"Rachel…Rachel…You know why. Because if you don't I'll make your life hell."

"I don't care if you make my life hell. I really don't care."

"Oh, please, Rachel. The matrons are onto the smoking. They're checking the fire escapes each night. I'm sorry I've been nasty. I really am. Mum says it's my default position. It's just what I do. Plus that Mandy Grogan gets me going. She's got it in for you. It's hard not to get involved, you know. I'm weak. I'm sorry. Please…"

"Ten it is," I said. She gave a pleading smile, said thanks (I hadn't seen this smile before…so unlike her…she was acting very oddly indeed), and shut my door gently.

Thank god she hadn't noticed her diary was missing. I went under the covers again and looked at the page I'd read. There were so many things about it that startled me. I was her friend! Taahnya was her enemy! She was moving in with Piers after school finished! She had a secret too big to write down! Add this to the stethoscope in her room (maybe she'd used this to check the baby was okay?) and I had suspect Number One.

I was absolutely sure it was her.

I didn't go to dinner. I put Amelia's diary back where I found it and thought hard about how to confront her. I waited till everyone got back, waited as everyone studied and showered and got ready for bed, took a puff of my ventolin and another two painkillers, and knocked on her door.

When she opened it, she had a green silk dressing gown on. Underneath I could see the frilly underwear set I'd found in her cupboard. It was red and lacy. "Can I talk to you, Amelia?"

She screwed up her face. The old horrible Amelia had returned already.

"I'm going to anyway," I said with unusual assertiveness, sliding the door shut behind me and sitting on her bed.

She was like, "What's wrong with you? You're white as a ghost."

"I have asthma, but that's not what I want to talk about."

"Whatever," she said, returning to the mirror to retouch her lips.

"Are you feeling okay?" I asked.

She didn't answer.

"Have you got anything you want to tell me?"

She didn't turn around.

"Amelia...I *know.*"

"What?" she said, turning to face me, her expression shocked, scared.

"I know what's happening and I want to help you."

She sat down on the bed beside me, floppy and weak, the silk of her dressing gown and the frills of her lingerie suddenly flat and formless.

"How'd you find out?"

"No one knows," I said. "I've taken care of things. But you need to decide what you're going to do now."

"I know. I know I do."

She started to cry. I found my arms lifting and hauling her in. I found myself holding the popular Amelia O'Donohue as she sobbed and sobbed in my arms.

"Do you want to talk about it?" I asked, not wanting to push her, not wanting to make her feel even worse.

"I do. I do, Rachel. I really do."

"Tell me."

"It started to get bad about six months ago. I found myself eating a lot more than before, feeling down…puking."

"It's okay," I said, as her tears fell on my shoulders.

"I prayed it'd go away. I prayed it'd just disappear, like, but it didn't. It got worse and worse. What'll happen if everyone finds out? What'll happen to me?"

"You have to go to the hospital."

"You think?"

"Yes."

"I don't want to. I don't want everyone to know."

"There's no way around it. You could be in danger. You must be hurting like mad."

"Not really…"

"Girls," Miss Rose announced over the loudspeaker. "Time for bed now. Sleep well, and don't be nervous. You'll all do really well tomorrow." The lights went out as soon as the announcement was finished.

"Shit!" Amelia said, moving away from my hug and coming-to suddenly. "Is that the time? Piers'll be here any second."

She picked up her mobile phone and checked he hadn't texted yet.

"Amelia, you have to deal with this now."

"No, I don't," she said, returning to her ice-queen former self.

"What does Piers think?"

"God, Piers doesn't know!"

"Really?"

"Now say it," she ordered.

"I don't need to say it. But I can't deal with this alone. It's not my problem. You have to fess up."

"Say it then piss off," she said.

So I did the usual cheek-slap, nose-pull, and recital, annoyed and amazed that this girl could be so self-centered and so screwed-up that she could just go on as if nothing had ever happened.

•••

When I got back to my room, the light of the baby monitor was flashing. I tiptoed downstairs with a saucepan of hot water. The television room was dark and quiet. Some girls were snoring. Some were giggling. I snuck in the darkroom, locked it behind me, fed the thing some warm milk, changed its nappy, and looked into its eyes.

He didn't look anything like Amelia O'Donohue, this boy

I'd named Sam. His eyes were blue. At first I thought this was strange, as Amelia and Piers both had brown eyes, but then I remembered that most newborns have blue eyes at first. It seemed sad that they would change, as blue eyes suited this baby somehow. Shiny little eyes that looked hard into mine. I had to go.

Amelia was still outside on the fire escape. I opened my window and took a look. jesus, wouldn't that *hurt?* She was unbelievable. I couldn't help but yell at her.

"Amelia, come in here now!"

A few moments later my door flew open.

"What the hell do you think you're doing?" she asked. "Who do you think you are?"

"I'm your friend and you need help."

"My friend! *Hardly*…And you're making a mountain out of a molehill," she said.

"A molehill?" I whispered, moving towards her angrily. "You've just given birth and you call it a molehill?"

"What?"

"Your baby needs you," I said.

"What are you talking about?"

"Amelia. You're confused. Remember our talk? I know all about it. I know everything. He's in the darkroom."

"Who?"

"The baby. *Your* baby."

"Rachel, are you mad?"

"Are *you?*"

"I asked you first," she said.

"No. I found your baby. In the linen cupboard."

"It's the medication. What are you on? Has the studying gotten to you?"

"It's not yours?" I asked.

"It's not anybody's, Rachel. It doesn't exist."

"Right, come with me," I said, grabbing her hand and dragging her to the second floor.

We'd almost reached the darkroom when Taahnya caught us. She was sneaking into the television room.

"Hey, Amelia, what are you doing?"

"Nothing," we both said at the same time.

"*All the Boys Love Mandy Lane's* on. You wanna watch? Or we could watch *CSI* if you'd rather."

"Maybe later," Amelia said.

"Yeah, maybe later," I said.

"Not you, retard," Taahnya said to me, one half of her lip curled so spectacularly that it almost touched her nostril. She shut the television door behind her.

I checked the hall. With no one in sight, I unlocked the door of the darkroom.

Once locked inside, I opened the cupboard door, turned on my flashlight and shone it at little Sam, lying there, eyes open, gurgling happily on his towel.

Thud.

Amelia had responded in the same way I had. I waved her unconscious face with my hand, slapping her cheek gently.

"Amelia! Amelia!"

She opened her eyes and stared at me for a second before the image flew back at her and she sat upright.

"What the fudge! There's a baby in the cupboard!"

"It's really not yours?"

"NO!"

"Then why did you tell me it was?"

"I didn't. I'm bulimic, idiot. I barf after dinner."

"So…if it's not yours…"

We both looked down at the little one, our faces huge against his. I'm sure he smiled at me.

"…then whose is it?"

"We have to tell Miss Rose," Amelia said.

"But the poor thing. Don't you think whoever the mother is might need someone to talk to first? What if she's terrified?

What if they take him from her? What if they send her to jail? Shouldn't we try and help her?"

"But she might be really sick."

"Tell you what," I said. "Let's see if we can find her tonight. One night. If we can't, we'll tell the teachers after assembly. Long as we know the baby's safe, and that no one's bleeding to death in the dorms, then there's no danger, is there? Just imagine how scared she must be."

"You're right," Amelia said. "Okay. One night."

"Deal. Right after my speech, we go to the office. Slap my cheek," I said. This was the first time I'd ever said those words. I was surprised that Amelia complied immediately. She slapped my cheek, pulled my nose and said: "If I tell, I'll go to hell."

CHAPTER
FIFTEEN

When we got back to the third floor, a group of girls were waiting in line outside my door.

The clinic. I'd forgotten I'd pinned a notice on the ground floor message board that afternoon, hoping the mother would come to me ALO to confess. It surprised me that people had responded—no one had sought my services for months. Must've been the onset of exams. People were tense and scared and needed someone to talk to. But lurking among them might be someone with a much bigger problem, I thought.

I grabbed Amelia and dragged her into the bathroom.

"Be my assistant," I said. "Maybe she's waiting to tell me."

"No one'll tell you anything if I'm there. I'm a Popular. That means no one trusts me, and everyone hates me."

"No one hates you."

"Everyone does!" she said, her eyes tearful.

"I don't."

She smiled at me. A genuine smile that traveled to her eyes. I'd never seen her smile like this before. It really suited her.

"Can you google from your phone?" I asked her.

"Aye."

"Then while I'm talking to people, get on the internet; see if you can find out what we should be looking out for."

She smiled again, much softer now than she'd ever been, and we made our way to our cubicles.

• • •

"Next!" I said, doctor-style. The girls were standing quietly outside, careful not to wake Miss Rose. A girl came in to confess that she was tempted to cheat in geography. I looked to see if she was unable to sit down properly, sore, feverish, or had swollen leaking nipples (blah!), but she didn't seem to have any obvious symptoms, and I dismissed her after advising her to think carefully before risking everything by cheating.

The next was Taahnya Jennings. I nearly died when she walked in. She'd never approached me for anything in her life.

She was like, "I haven't got a secret. I'm here to warn you not to take Amelia from me. She's my best friend. We're Populars, yeah. You're, like, a retard. Got it?"

I looked her over. If what I'd heard was true, she'd been pregnant once already. Had she done it again? Had she waited too long this time and been left with no choice but to give birth?

"Got it?" She repeated. I hadn't answered her. I was looking at her skirt to see if there was any red anywhere.

"I've got it. But can I ask you something first?"

"I might not answer."

"I'll take the risk. Have you been feeling okay today?"

"What?"

"Has anything happened to you today that you want to talk about?"

She decided not to answer, curled her lip in disgust, and left.

After Taahnya, Mohawk Vanessa came in. Stories about her sexuality had continued throughout the year. Mandy, Louisa, and Aimee had told everyone Vanessa was angry at the world and on a mission to convert the straights and that they'd regularly heard her and Jill from the fourth floor (Right) in the middle of the night making kissing and other noises. She sat opposite me, picking the skin around her fingernails. To ease her nerves, I started the conversation.

"Did you tell the person?"

"What?" she asked.

"You know, last time you were here you said you loved someone and wondered if you should tell them."

"Oh, yeah. That. Nah. Well yeah. But that's not what I want to talk about…This is like big time top secret. Big time…"

I'd only spoken to Vanessa that one time and hadn't noticed the way she talked. She didn't sound like an angry marginalized person.

"Right, so I'm just gonna like blurt it out…I saw Miss Rose kiss the chef in the kitchen last night. She was crying afterwards."

"Really?" I was gob smacked.

"Aye. Like proper kissing. Tongues and shit."

"He's married though, yeah?" I asked.

"His wife's a cow, apparently. Jill heard her call him a prick in the driveway once."

"Blimey, listen. I don't think we should say anything to anyone about this. Can you keep it to yourself? I'd hate to get her into trouble. She's the best thing there is about this place."

Vanessa agreed. She loved Miss Rose too. "She's a top bird," she said.

When Vanessa left, it made me think.

Miss Rose.

CHAPTER
SIXTEEN

When the line of girls dissipated, Amelia came back in.
"Any luck?"

"Miss Rose is getting it on with the chef."

"Really? Worth following up. But she's rake thin."

"Some women hardly show at all," I said. "Depends on your body shape. You find anything online?"

"Not much. Check this out," Amelia said. "Let's fill these in and narrow it down."

Amelia placed several A3 sheets of paper on my bed. At the top of each was a heading:

CHERRY TARTS

GIRLS WITH BOYFRIENDS

GIRLS WHO WOULD HAVE DONE IT AROUND NINE MONTHS AGO

GIRLS WHO MIGHT NOT KNOW ABOUT CONTRACEPTION

ALWAYS FAT GIRLS

SUDDENLY FAT GIRLS

SCREWED UP GIRLS

STRESSED OUT GIRLS

SICK OR BLEEDING OR UNABLE TO WALK GIRLS

OFF SCHOOL A LOT GIRLS

"Why stressed out girls?" I asked.

"According to the internet, the girl may not even be aware herself."

"What do you mean?"

"Look at this," she said, handing me her phone. On screen was an extract she'd found online. I read it out loud.

"Denied pregnancy describes a lack of subjective awareness of pregnancy until the end of gestation in pregnant women. Very often, bodily symptoms of pregnancy (nausea, amenorrhea, and abdomen swelling) are absent or greatly reduced, and neonates tend to be underweight: in many cases pregnancy goes undetected also by relatives and physicians."

"What site is this from?" I asked cynically. "Wikipedia?"

"No, no, this is not a bam up. It's from like a proper medical journal. Look at this one; they sometimes call it splitting…" Amelia clicked onto another article.

"Psychiatrists call this ability to separate yourself from

reality 'splitting.' This is a mental mechanism, which results when a person is under very, very great stress, and instead of dealing with that distress and the very high level of anxiety, they split it off from consciousness. The minute you talk about it to somebody else it becomes real. Whereas, as long as the process of concealment, denial, and splitting goes on, it remains a fantasy."

She'd also printed out a true story about a nineteen-year-old girl who was seriously freakin' out about life. She wanted to hide it so much that she had no physical symptoms. She gave birth to a baby girl in her bedroom then chucked her in a rubbish bin and made an anonymous call to the porter. The poor girl was arrested and given five years probation. "See," Amelia said when I was done reading. "It could be like a mental problem. Like she's so stressed and stuff that she might have hidden it from everyone, even from herself. Just ignore it, pretend it's not there."

"But how could you hide labor?"

"Maybe some kind of mad episode. Or maybe the shock left her clueless. I dunno. Anyway, we should keep an open mind."

We filled out the A3 sheets using the knowledge we already had. Amelia turned out to be a minefield of information when it came to cherry tarts (though her criterion seemed a bit dodgy to me—for example, Becky from the first floor was excellent at putting a condom on a cucumber and Roberta from the fourth floor walked funny). She told me something I already knew—that the girl with the ponytail had regular liaisons with the cute, ex-footballer-PE teacher, Mr. Burns, in the woods. She also told me that Louisa MacDonald had done it with a Baltyre boy at the last school dance.

But looking over our completed sheets, we realized that our methodical approach had hardly narrowed down the search at all. Almost every girl in the school fell under one or more of our categories.

We decided to knock on every cubicle door, pretending to need a painkiller or something, take a mental note of anything unusual, then reconvene in my room.

I had the third and fourth floors.

• • •

But oh god, this asthma was killing me. The nebulizer the nurse had given me after I fainted had provided some relief, but it was surfacing again, that feeling that someone had put a pillow over my head and was pressing down so hard that some of the feathers had made their way into my throat. Perched on the edge of my bed, I puffed on my ventolin again. After a few minutes of imagining myself in a calm, airy, painless place

(Edinburgh Uni Halls! Cycling through Amsterdam! On a train to Moscow!), I put on my dressing gown and headed to the fourth floor.

It was well after 11:00. Most of the girls were asleep, but after forty minutes, I managed to wake enough of them up to gain sixteen aspirin, at least a dozen expletives, a few "sorry, don't haves," and one seriously big suspect.

Her name was Viv. She was in my English class. Her stomach was so large it leaked loosely from between her pajama top and bottom. Her face was gray with lack of blood. And she was so hostile to the intrusion—"I said get out, I'm sleeping!"—that I just *knew*. I raced down to the third floor to find Amelia in my room.

"What do you know about Viv Metstein?" I said.

Her face glowed with excitement and she cross-referenced the sheets we'd filled in earlier…"Suddenly fat, pale, stressed out…"

"All of the above. What should we do?"

She was like, "Spy!"

"Should we not just ask her?"

"*No!* What if we're wrong? She'd tell everyone. We have to be sure."

We waited long enough for Viv to have fallen asleep again. In the meantime, Amelia—using the skills she'd honed from

Crime Scene Investigation—prepared herself to sweep all other relevant scenes for evidence.

I stood guard as she rummaged through the linen cupboard. I'd been so shocked that I hadn't noticed anything but the baby. But, in fact, the towels and sheets were covered in clues.

There was blood on several of the towels.

A red sodden pair of pants was under a sheet.

And there was a huge wet lump double wrapped in pillow-cases. Without thinking, we peeked in the open end…

…then ran to the bathroom to puke.

Amelia was like, "Oh jesus, what was *that?*"

"The cord and placenta," I said. "Whoever it was, she obviously knew how to deal with it. Waited a while, clamped it, cut it…"

Several dry-retches later, we hid the towels and offending insides in an old bag in my room, and rinsed the underpants in one of the shower cubicles. Once they were gunk free, we examined them.

White. Asda. Brief. Not labeled. Size eight. Nothing extraor-dinary. But it narrowed it down to size eight girls on a budget with non-labeling type mothers.

Still could be Viv Metstein. She was flabby, but she always wore clothes that were too small—T-shirts that curled up above her belly button; low jeans and tracksuit pants that cut a line underneath her wobbly tummy; bras that oozed boob from the edges.

The next piece of evidence to examine was the baby himself. Did he look like Viv Metstein? Did he have her large ears and translucent skin?

We snuck down to the darkroom together and stared at the baby. He did not have large ears. They were tiny and cute, like dried apricots pinned back against his perfect-shaped noggin. He did not have peely-wally skin. In fact, his seemed deliciously sallow. He did not look anything like Viv Metstein.

"Could take after the father," I said.

"He's just too pretty," Amelia said.

"Let's check her room anyways."

We crept up to the fourth floor, and gently slid open her cubicle door.

She was snoring, her mouth open and ugly. She was clinging onto a pink teddy bear.

Using my flashlight, I leafed through a pile of papers on her desk. Revision notes for our English exam, letters from home… One piece of paper was folded and crumpled. I opened it, careful not to make too much noise, and put my hand over my mouth. It was an information sheet from the family planning clinic.

Next, I opened her cupboard and pointed my flashlight

towards her smalls—but they weren't small, they were huge. Pink. Marks and Spencer's. Size twelve. And labeled.

Hmm.

• • •

"I need ice cream!" Amelia said as we tiptoed down from the fourth floor. "Follow me!"

I did as I was told, trailing behind her down to the ground floor, across the walkway, and to the side of the dining hall.

"Give me a leg up!" Amelia ordered. We were standing underneath a small window, which was open about an inch.

"We can't!" I said. "We'll get into trouble."

"Just do it," she said. "If I don't eat, I'm no use."

Reluctantly, I cupped my hands and used the little strength I had to heave her foot up towards the window, which she expertly pushed open and climbed through. A few seconds later, the side door to the kitchen opened.

"Welcome to my world," she said, ushering me inside and closing the door behind her. It was dark inside, but Amelia knew how to find her way around. She grabbed my hand, taking two spoons from the cutlery tray en route, and walked me towards a large steel door.

She let us in, closed the door behind her, and fumbled in the dark for a moment.

"Ta-da!" she said, the flickering light of two small candles revealing our location.

It was a fridge. It was bigger than my cubicle, and filled to the brim with buckets and boxes of food: meatballs in tomato sauce, soup, pasties, Bolognese, partially cooked pasta, lettuce, bread, sprinkles, Flakes, raspberry sauce, wafers, waffles…

"Check this," she said, opening one of the freezers at the back. Inside were tubs and tubs of ice cream. She took a foot-high tub out of the freezer, poured a stupid amount of sprinkles on top, then lashings of thick red raspberry sauce, then grabbed a can of scooshy cream from a shelf, and scooshed ten inches of white sugar fluff onto the top. To finish off, she stuck ten Flakes around the edges like birthday candles, handed me a spoon, and said, "Bottoms up!"

"It's freezing!" I said, taking a small spoonful of ice cream.

"Here," she said, grabbing two expensive-looking sleeping bags from the back of the top shelf. "I hide them here for moments like this."

"You do this often?" I asked, zipping myself into the down-filled mummy.

"Maybe."

"Is there enough air?"

"I stayed five hours one time. There's a wee grate at the top…See."

Indeed there was.

Satisfied that I wasn't going to freeze or suffocate to death, I took a spoonful of ice cream. But I felt too breathless and sick to eat.

Somehow, our illegal candlelit refuge felt intimate and safe. Bar Amelia's frantic gobbling, we were comfortably silent.

After a while I said, "Will you chuck this up after?"

"I'll try not to."

"Why do you do that?"

"That's the biggie. The one my folks pay Dr. Halliday to figure out. Apparently I have low self-esteem."

"You?"

"Hard to believe, isn't it? I dunno if it's true. All I know is it makes me feel better, for a while anyway."

"Why don't you feel good? You should. You're gorgeous, rich, clever, popular."

Amelia had gobbled an impressive ditch into the tub of ice cream. She put it down and sighed. "All I know is sometimes I feel like a spaceship has dropped me down here from another planet."

This made me smile. I paused before I said what was on my mind. "I know *exactly* what you mean."

Amelia smiled at me and it melted the frost on my face. Other than Sammy, she was the first person to look at me as if she understood me. If I wasn't a miserable pent-up Scot, I might have hugged her and told her I was so glad we were friends now. Instead I said, "We'd better go. We've got lots to do."

Amelia put the tub of desecrated ice cream back in the freezer, and said, "Right, Detective Inspector Ross. Let's solve this thing."

CHAPTER
SEVENTEEN

M iss Rose had a cubicle in the middle of my floor. Her
walls went all the way to the ceiling. Her door had a
lock. It wasn't going to be easy. In fact, it was going to be risky.
But Amelia had an idea.

"You ask her for help," she said, "then I'll sneak in while she's
talking to you."

It was genius.

I knocked on her door. Then knocked again. Eventually, Miss
Rose appeared wearing a white dressing gown. Her short thick
hair seemed traumatized from her time in bed. It stuck up wide
and round like an excited peacock.

"Rachel, are you all right?"

"Actually, I'm not. I'm so sorry to wake you."

"You didn't wake me…I was reading."

I didn't have to lie. I was feeling dreadful. My breathing
was becoming more labored again—probably not helped by

spending an hour in a fridge—and a fever had taken over my head so that even my hair felt sore.

"My goodness, you're burning up," she said. "When did you last have painkillers?"

It had been six hours since my last dose, and as soon as she mentioned it, I felt desperate for the pain to be covered over, for my aching head and body to be soothed.

"It's one hundred and two," Miss Rose said, looking at the ear thermometer in the medical room. She'd put the nebulizer on. Masked and stationary, I realized just how terrible my condition had become. I wasn't sure if I'd ever be able to stand up again.

"Rachel, I think you should go to the hospital."

I used the same argument with her that I used with Amelia about the baby. "Please, just give me till morning. If I'm no better, I'll go, I promise."

She agreed in the end and tucked me into my bed like my mother used to do when I was little, when I called her Mummy, when we lived in Edinburgh, before she told me a secret and the good lord took away all loveliness.

"Here," she said, handing me a carton of apple juice and directing the straw into my mouth. "You must keep your fluids up, honey."

As the liquid made its way down my throat, Miss Rose gently moved the hair away from my forehead. Soothed by her gentle attention, I found myself wondering if someone as caring as she was could ever abandon a baby.

As soon as Miss Rose left my cubicle, Amelia stormed in.

She was like, "Omygod! Omygod! Omygod!"

"What? Tell me. Show me!"

She had an envelope in her hand. "You are not going to believe this."

"Show me!" I said, dragging my aching limbs and struggling lungs from out of my snug tucked-in-edness.

Amelia opened the envelope and took out a small note, the kind that usually comes attached to flowers.

"*My love, we'll be together soon. I'm going to tell her tonight, Px*"

"It came with roses," Amelia said. "P for Pete…the chef."

We had several suspects now: the girl with the ponytail, who'd allegedly done it with the PE teacher; Viv Metstein, who'd recently visited the family planning clinic; Taahnya, who'd allegedly been pregnant once before; and Miss Rose, who was having an affair with our married chef.

"What do we do next?" I asked.

Amelia decided we should look on MSN and Facebook, see if we could find out anything more about our suspects.

It was after two in the morning. I was exhausted and ill, but using Amelia's iPhone, we methodically checked the social networks of our suspects and as many other girls as we could remember. We discovered that nearly half those on social networks did quizzes, posted photographs, wrote in text speak, and defined themselves as being "in a relationship." Most of them spoke at length about what boys had said and what they were planning to wear that night—for example, the latest exchange between Taahnya and Mandy: "*He said that? Gasp! Ime wearin my jeggings n sleeveless blue top n hoodieeee…*" "*What the fudge! Jeggings! But meee tooo. By the way, do you know macaroons have potato in them?*" None of them had posted anything that might help us find who had the baby.

"Let's have an emergency clinic after breakfast," I said. "We'll ask cryptic questions."

"Good idea." Amelia yawned. "Let's devise a questionnaire and see if we can catch them out."

"They might not answer," I said, silently adding: *especially Taahnya and Viv.*

"Pretend it's for your talk tomorrow. For research. Y'know, questions like: What was the hardest part of your academic year?"

She dictated several other questions:

Did any unexpected incidents make life at school difficult?

What do you want to do when you leave school?

Did any health issues concern you?

Have you been able to talk to someone if something is worrying you?

I was writing these down when the monitor light went on. I turned the volume dial on low so I could hear if the baby was crying. To my surprise, he wasn't, but someone was whispering. Oh my god, I'd left the key in the door after checking the baby last time. Someone was in the darkroom.

CHAPTER
EIGHTEEN

know!" someone said over the monitor. "Let's steal her revision notes."

"Good idea. We could hide them in the sewing room," the second girl said.

"Or throw them away," the first said. "Retard boy-tease. You see what she wore to that dance?"

"I know. Quiz is *so* gay."

Amelia and I recognized the voices at the same time. Mandy Grogan and Taahnya Scot, our ex-best friends. They were obviously talking about me, a need to torment me reinvigorated by my growing friendship with Amelia O'Donohue.

I turned the monitor's volume off, and we headed downstairs, then stopped at the door to the darkroom. We pressed our ears against the door—they were still talking, but the baby hadn't woken, thank god. I opened the door, scaring Mandy and Taahnya to death.

"jesus christ!" Mandy said.

"You girls planning something?" Amelia said.

Taahnya was like, "Whatever."

"We heard you," I said.

Taahnya looked at Mandy, and then at Amelia. She made a quick decision. Switch alliances.

"Not me. It's Mandy," Taahnya said, looking at Mandy, with whom she'd been hitherto conniving. And at that moment, I felt kind of sorry for her. She was obviously so desperately in awe of Amelia O'Donohue, so in need of her love and devotion, that she'd do anything, hurt anyone, to win her affection.

"Why don't you tell Rachel here why you've been such a bitch since the September weekend?" Taahnya said to Mandy, her change of sides now complete.

Mandy was dumbstruck. How had the tide changed so suddenly?

While I wanted to know more than anything what Mandy had done behind my back this time, all I could think about was the baby. He was in the cupboard, just behind the dirty little rats. Sleeping, hopefully. But he might not be sleeping. He might be sick. He might be dead. He might have stopped breathing while I was on some stupid investigation or eating some stupid ice cream in some stupid kitchen fridge.

"I don't care," I said. "Just please get out of this room." *Please*

please please please leave this room, I was thinking. *Amelia, have you forgotten who's in the cupboard?*

"I want you to know what your best friend did to you, Rachel," Taahnya said. "I want you to know why she's been so mean."

"Shut up," Mandy said, her lips trembling with worry.

"I don't care. I really don't. I just want you to get out. Please!" I looked at Amelia, then at the cupboard door. My eyes were saying, *goddsake, get them out of here!*

"Rachel's right," Amelia said. "Get out. We can talk about it another time."

Taahnya did as she was asked, leaving the room in a huff, her copycat teddy floating behind her.

But Mandy refused to leave. Who was she? This school had turned her into an evil alien. "You've turned so boring since you came here," she said. "All you do is study. You're like some hermit."

"It's guilt," Amelia said. "Guilt makes you mean."

Mandy was like, "Shut up, Amelia. What do you know?"

"I know you slept with Rachel's boyfriend that first time you went home. Taahnya told me. I know you've been dating him ever since."

"John?" I asked.

"Aye, John," Mandy said, her eyes cruel. She pushed her floppy wool turtleneck down to reveal a grotesque love-bite as evidence.

"I really don't care. I just want you to leave this room!"

"He says he loves me. He says you're a slut."

For a moment, I forgot about baby Sam. I forgot that just behind Mandy a little boy was sleeping, hopefully. I stared at her, wondering who she was. How could she be so cruel?

A cat noise.

"What was that?" Mandy asked.

Amelia and I stared at each other and closed the door to the darkroom.

Sammy was making noises. Nice ones, not crying, he was talking baby talk.

"A cat," I said.

Another noise. Definitely not a cat.

"There it is again," Mandy said, moving towards the cupboard. I stood in front of it, my arms outstretched, desperate to stop her finding him.

"I don't care about John," I said. "But you must leave this room NOW."

"I will not," she said, pushing me out of the way and trying to open the cupboard door.

There was a struggle. Her yanking me this way, that, trying to grab the handle. Me holding her back. Amelia pushing against the cupboard door so it'd stay closed.

It was a noisy struggle, one that made Sam's happy sounds turn to crying.

"Holy shit," Mandy yelled, recognizing the noises and forcing the door open with all her strength.

The three of us stood before the cupboard, watching little Sam watch us, his body twitching baby twitches, his eyes firmly on mine.

"What the fudge! Whose…what…how…" Mandy mumbled.

"We don't know," Amelia said. "We're trying to find out. It's not yours?" she asked.

"Of course not. Bloody hell. Call the matron. Call the police!"

I picked up Sam and cuddled him. He was quiet now.

"We will, in the morning. We just want to find out whose it is first, give the poor girl a chance and some support. Do you think it could be Taahnya's?"

"No. She's a virgin!"

"She is not. She had an abortion," Amelia said.

"She didn't. Her big sister made that up to get back at her for staining her favorite T-shirt. She's a real bitch, her sister. But now Taahnya likes that everyone thinks she did. Makes her seem cool, she says. Don't tell her I said. She made me promise not to tell."

"Ever the faithful friend," I quipped.

"Shut up. What do you know about friends? You haven't got any."

"Yes she has," Amelia said, taking us both by surprise.

Mandy looked at Amelia, shocked, then continued, "Whatever. This is serious. The girl who had this baby abandoned him! She should go to jail. The kid should go into care! We should call social services, that's who."

At this, I handed Sam to Amelia and moved towards Mandy, my poise and facial expression enough to scare her into walking backwards into the wall.

"We will not do that."

"We have to," she said. "This girl's crazy. She's dangerous. She doesn't deserve our help."

Before I knew it, I had pushed my forearm into Mandy's stomach, pressed her so hard against the wall that she couldn't move, taken the neck of her turtleneck jumper and lifted it up over her head.

"What are you doing? Stop it!"

I didn't. I grabbed a stapler from the old trestle table under the window and stapled her turtleneck together above her head. One two three four, she was now a wrapped-up toffee apple.

"What are you doing?" Amelia said, scared.

"We've got to put her somewhere till morning." We both knew where.

CHAPTER NINETEEN

As we snuck back from the kitchen, a distant sun was turning the sky to blue-gray. Time was running out. As if to add to the tick tick ticking clock, when we got to my cubicle, the baby monitor was flashing.

"I can't go," Amelia said, "I can't stay awake. Can you deal with him? We can get up early and get on with the plan."

Our plan was a good one. At breakfast, I would make an announcement. An emergency clinic would be held in my room, where I would ask our cryptic questions, then—if we were still uncertain—I would make my speech and then go to the office and tell the teachers.

Something peculiar happened when I went down to the darkroom. Perhaps the flu asthma fanfare had made me delirious. I don't know. But I found myself unable to leave Sam. He was bright red from crying when I got there, and it seemed to take hours for the bottle to warm to the right temperature, but when I gave him the milk, he transformed into the epitome of gorgeousness, sucking away while staring into my eyes. I couldn't help but stare back, captivated by this tiny boy, this tiny unwanted secret.

He seemed to work on me like ventolin, calming my breathing, soothing me.

And I couldn't leave him. As much as I knew I should, as much as I knew I needed to look over my English notes and get at least two hours' sleep, I couldn't. So I lay on the floor of the darkroom with a little baby called Sam nuzzling into my tummy; watching as he slept; cuddling him if he seemed cold; and time, worry, everything stood still.

I think we both woke when the radio came on at 7:00 a.m. and Miss Rose said, "Good morning, girls!" over the intercom.

I fed, changed, and wrapped him, kissed him on the forehead, then locked the door, careful to take the key with me this time, and snuck back up to my room. It was crunch time.

Crunch—Whose was this baby? Whose was this huge secret?

Crunch—English exam. My first concrete step towards freedom.

• • •

Oh God, the asthma. The pain. The head. The stress. I found myself on the floor, praying. *Dear god, even though I don't believe in you, please can you let me do well in my exams? Please can you let me find this poor scared girl? Please can she be okay? Please can he be okay? Please can I be okay? To the power of infinity. Amen.*

• • •

Praying reminded me of my mother. Not long ago, she would have loved to see me praying voluntarily on the hardwood floor of my cubicle. It would have pleased her no end. She would have smiled. She would have assumed I wanted to be saved. She would have been proud that her daughter had finally found the same misery she had since leaving the city. Would she feel the same now? I wasn't so sure. During the christmas holiday, she seemed to have changed. She didn't seem as preoccupied with the good lord. Dare I say? She seemed happy.

I could see girls making their way over for breakfast.

The English notes on my desk beckoned, so I tried to read them, but they continued to whirl around the page and I couldn't make head or tail of them. I don't know why, but I found myself getting an old shoe box from my cupboard and touching the unopened letters my mother had sent.

Not just touching. Opening.

Not just opening. Reading.

CHAPTER
TWENTY

September 28th

Dear Rachel,

As soon as you left I regretted it. Not just letting you go, my darling girl, but our life here. The life you hate so much and yearn to escape.

We went to church yesterday and no one spoke to us. I don't understand.

Oh Rach, we missed you so much last weekend. Camping without you is no fun.

Please ring me. Please write to me. Please talk to me when I visit.

I love you,

Mum.

• • •

October 12th

Dear Rachel,

At last I have spoken to your father. Spoken properly, without any of the guilt and sadness I've felt since coming here. I feel really bad about this but I think we needed this time alone so we could face things, be honest with each other. You know it's not easy trying to get on with a teenager. It's not easy being thought of as a "retard." (You really shouldn't use that word, Rach. It's a word that should never be used.) It makes you forget who you are. We needed to get to know each other again. We talked about the problems we had in Edinburgh. His work. My loneliness. Leaving it too late to have a sibling for you, someone for you to play with, laugh with. I told him outright. We must move on. We must forgive and forget. Please, I said. It was a dark time and we went and made it darker. We thought the island and the church would fix things. But they didn't.

He cried. He reminded me of how happy we were in the city, before his job took him away all the time. Remember we used to argue for ages over who'd have the last Tunnock's tea cake? Remember we used to have family cuddles, so soft and delicious, we'd all melt into each other for ages? Remember you used to call us the old fogies?

He loves you. You know that? We are both sorry now. We feel we have driven you away.

We love you,

Mum and Dad

• • •

November 3rd

Dear Rachel,

Why will you not talk to me? I don't want to push myself on you. I don't want to ruin your dreams, your huge magnificent dreams—I'm so proud of you for having them. I had them once. I wanted to be an actress!

Please, please talk to me.

Forgive me.

We love you,

Mum and Dad

• • •

January 7th

Dear Rachel,

It was so lovely having you home for Christmas. I wish you'd seemed happier to be here. Are you feeling okay? Are you *really* okay?

Last night at church the minister's sermon seemed to be directed at us. When I looked into his eyes afterwards, I saw badness.

Can someone like that really save us?

We love you,

Mum and Dad

• • •

March 22nd

Dearest darling Rachel,

I miss you. I long to read you a story at night and tuck you in.

Do you get my messages? Miss Rose always says she can't seem to find you when I call. I know you're avoiding us. I'm not sure what to do about it.

Have we lost you forever? It feels like we have. It's made us see things clearly.

We don't say prayers any more, my love. We don't go to church.

We believe in good. But there doesn't seem to be any here.

We both feel the same way.

We love you,

Mum and Dad

• • •

April 26th

My little girl,

I'm going to leave you alone till your exams are over. I know how much it means to you. But please know that we support you.

We have forgiven and forgotten. We have moved on, sold the farm.

We've put in an offer for a three bedroom flat in the West End of Glasgow. It's on the second floor. It has a view of the

176

University of Glasgow and the Kelvingrove Art Galleries. At night, the buildings light the sky. It's truly beautiful.

Dad's starting a new job in the city in a month. He's going to be a reporter on the news! I have an interview next week. Rachel, I am so sick of sheep.

I understand if you want to live with friends, or in student accommodation, but the offer is there.

The new life is there.

Our old family will be there,

We love you,

Mum and Dad

CHAPTER
TWENTY-ONE

My mum was back. Not my mother, but my mum. And my dad. I now remembered the endless arguments we had over the last tea cake, all three of us hovering over it, presenting our arguments as to why we should be the one to get it.

I am little and I need to grow, I would say.

I am large and I can beat you up, Dad would say.

I will pay you each £5, and Mum would get the tea cake.

I remembered our cuddles—on the sofa, in bed, at the front door when I'd returned from school or Dad had returned from work. I remembered Dad used to take me to the park in Edinburgh, laughing as he piggybacked me through the gardens. I remembered that Mum used to make up plays in our flat. I would always be the princess and she would be the queen. I remembered I used to call them the old fogies, and they'd laugh like crazy then cuddle into each other and Mum'd say, "I love you, old fogie," and Dad'd say, "And I love you, old fogie."

I remembered how lonely Mum was when Dad worked

abroad. So lonely I could hear her crying at night when I was supposed to be sleeping.

I remembered the fight she had with Dad before he went away that last time.

"You can't leave me here!" she'd begged. "I can't cope without you! Take us with you, please."

I remembered him ringing, her refusing to talk to him. "She's busy," I'd lie for her.

I remembered the new friend.

The bathtub.

The pinky promise.

Daddy coming home, at long last, to surprise us. "I've taken another job!" he said, hugging my mum. "I'm going to work here in the Edinburgh office. I'm so sorry."

The celebratory meal afterwards. Lemonade and black-currant for me. Lots of wine for them.

And later that night, Mum tucking me into bed, happy-tears in her eyes.

Dad coming in afterwards, kissing me, saying, "I love you, my poppet. I love you so much. I'm sorry things have been tough. They're going to get better. I'm going to be home every night from now on."

"So you're not going to get a divorce?" I asked.

"Of course not."

"And Mummy won't run away with the little red man?"

"Sorry?"

"The man she has bubble baths with."

• • •

Loud fights. Tears. Doors banging. Long walks. A move to the island. Maybe the good lord would fix things.

We locked ourselves in a wet world without temptation. It was called forgiveness. It was called a fresh start. But it was neither of those things.

It was death for me, yes. But mostly, for them.

Mum had never blamed me. "It's not your fault," she'd whispered as we'd looked out of the ferry window as it approached our prison, our belongings crammed in a hired van on the deck.

But it was my fault. I'd told a secret. I'd ruined our lives.

We never spoke of it again. I whined and moaned about our new circumstances. Mum and Dad sank deeper into their depression, waiting to be saved by the good lord.

Why had I been so scathing of them as they battled their own demons? Why had I only seen my own unhappiness?

I would ring Mum and Dad as soon as English was over. I'd talk to them, properly. I'd tell them that the idea of a bedroom overlooking Glasgow University (where I would go, if I got in…) would make me the happiest girl in the world.

But first things first. Breakfast…

And cryptic questions.

CHAPTER
TWENTY-TWO

That morning, I understood how frail elderly people might feel when putting on tights. There were so many steps involved. Turning them from inside-out to outside-in. Gathering one leg into my hand, stretching it over my foot, up my leg, oh dear, a snag—the process went on and on and on. And the buttons on my shirt appeared too big for the holes. By the time I'd dressed for breakfast I had to rest for a while before walking all the way downstairs and across the walkway to the dining hall. *Had the walkway changed?* I wondered as I willed myself to make it to the end. It seemed darker, the wooden trellis-style fence that edged it seemed more oppressive, like it was slowly moving inwards to crush me. I felt so sick I had to stop several times en route, but when Miss Rose saw me, I picked my shoulders up and pretended to be fine.

"How are you?" she asked. "Do you want me to fix that tie?"

I looked down and noticed I'd merely looped it around

my shoulders. Knotting it and tucking in my shirt, I realized that, despite great effort, I'd made a right mess of getting dressed.

Miss Rose looked very different from the night before. Her hair had settled around the contours of her high cheekbones. Her hippyish free-flowing skirt billowed below one of those empire-line tops that make most people look pregnant— GASP—but the top was so loose it was impossible to tell what her stomach might be shaped like underneath. If there was a post-birth swelling under there, I couldn't see it.

"All better!" I said, checking out the boobs I'd never noticed before (large, round, not leaking as far as I could see) and then (remembering the questions we'd devised) added, "What about you? Are you feeling okay? Is there anything you'd like to tell me?"

"What?" she asked

"I just wondered...sometimes teachers...matrons...need to be looked after too. You're so good to us, Miss Rose. So good, and I appreciate it."

"Well thank you, Rachel, but there's nothing..."

"Nothing at all?"

She looked at me suspiciously then said very matter-of-factly, "Nothing."

. . .

When I got into the dining hall, all the girls were either seated or in the queue for toast. I stood at the front of the hall and banged a spoon against a plate. It took a few more bangs before everyone stopped and listened.

"It has come to my attention that someone in this room may require my services. As a result, an emergency *If I Tell* clinic will take place in my cubicle till the bell rings for assembly."

. . .

I wasn't hungry. In fact, I felt nauseated and faint and breathless. I just had a few more hurdles: the clinic, the assembly, the exam. Oh god, the exam. I was never going to blitz it at this rate. I sighed loudly as I staggered across to the dorms and almost collapsed when I got to my cubicle.

I lay on the bed, waiting for the culprit to arrive. Surely my announcement would make it clear that we knew. Surely she would come.

The clock ticked in the hall. The washing machine buzzed. Girls came back to the dorms to get their bags, their voices flitting in and out of earshot.

No one came.

It was 8:15. The assembly would start in three quarters of an hour.

I dragged myself from my bed, put on my cardigan and blazer, and noticed the flashing light.

Shite, he was awake.

● ● ●

Oh little boy. Little boy! Smiling already. Should he smile already? Was he smiling at me? I touched the fine brown hair on his soft head as he drank, waiting till the last drop of milk had disappeared from the bottle. I then changed his nappy, kissed his forehead, locked the room, put the key in my blazer pocket, and walked as fast as I could downstairs.

It must have been after 8:30. The dorms were practically empty. On the first floor, Miss Craig was packing up the medical equipment to begin her research work for the day.

"How are you feeling?" she asked.

"Much better…Did many girls come in this morning?" I asked, hoping the mother had sought help.

"None. Would you believe it? I think exam adrenaline's keeping the bugs away."

"You're probably right," I said, sad that she hadn't had the courage to come forward yet, but happy that this meant she was probably doing okay. I made my way downstairs to the ground floor…

…to see my mother, running towards the building.

CHAPTER
TWENTY-THREE

My little girl!" she said, racing towards me and taking me in her arms. "You're so sick. Oh dear, Rachel, you need help."

"I'm fine," I said, breaking the hug. I didn't have time for this. I knew I needed to sort things out with her, but not now. I had so many other things to do.

She was like, "You're not fine. You're deathly white. And your buttons are all wrong!"

I looked at my cardigan. Indeed I had done it all wrong.

"Mum, I do feel okay, I promise. I really need to go."

"Give me five minutes," she said. "Sit here with me. Five minutes. Tops."

I sighed then sat on the bottom step. She sat about four inches away from me. It felt like a mile.

"Are you nervous?" she said after an awkward pause.

"I was. I don't know what I am now."

"I wanted to give you this," she said, handing me an envelope. I opened it quickly, desperate for these five minutes to end so I could deal with the whole baby in the cupboard/speech/exam madness.

Darling Rachel, it read,

Good luck with your exams. We're dying to have you home again. A different, better home. It's even bigger than the flat in Edinburgh.

Mumxxx

On the other side, Dad had scrawled,

We love you Rachel. There's nothing holding you back now. Or us! Dadxxx

I put the card back in the envelope. "Mum? I have to confess something."

"What?" Her eyes were wide open with worry. I realized I'd been over-dramatic.

"Oh, it's nothing big, just…I didn't read your letters till last night."

There was a pause. Mum put her hand on mine.

"You wrote that you and Dad needed time alone. So…you were glad to get rid of me." I didn't want to look at her for some reason.

"Of course not. I didn't mean that. I just meant we needed some space to get over…you know…"

"You shagging some garden gnome."

"Well, yes…and after you told Dad…"

"Like *I'm* the baddy."

"I'm doing this all wrong, aren't I? Of course you're not the baddy. I was. But I have to be honest and admit I did feel angry back then. You know, part of me thought if you hadn't told then maybe everything would have been okay. I never loved that man. Not even sure I liked him. I was…I guess I was weak and lonely and stupid. I'm so sorry I ever put you in that position." She *made* me look into her eyes, holding both my hands in both hers, holding them up high, reducing the four inches between us to nothing.

"Now I know that things wouldn't have been okay. The guilt would have tortured me. Rachel, *I* would have told your father. I would have had to."

She was tearing up. "I love you so much."

She looked much prettier all vulnerable like this. And I hadn't noticed till now, but for the first time in years she wasn't dressed in old jeans and a woolly jumper. She had a striking patterned dress on and patent leather boots. Her mouth was loose and relaxed. Her cheeks had color. She wasn't sighing and starting into space. She was looking at me, really looking.

"Do you?" I guess I wanted to hear her say it again.

"I love you. You are my beautiful, clever, funny, *determined*— and did I say *beautiful*—daughter."

Thankfully, I hadn't managed to put mascara on that morning. If I had, it'd have drawn a black-smudge highway all the way to my neck. She wiped a tear from my cheek.

"And I love your father too. He's the love of my life, you know. I made a terrible mistake back then, but we're going to be good now. We're going to be great, and I want you to promise me you'll never blame yourself for what happened. No one should ever ask you to keep a secret. I should never have asked. It's not fair. It's destructive. It wasn't your fault."

When we hugged, it felt alien at first, like a diary entry re-read years after the writing, once so familiar and full of emotion, now just words on a page. But then I melted into her and I remembered the feelings I once had as they came crashing into the present. I'd been so alone for so long, and I could feel it changing. I could feel myself opening up, un-bottling, letting her in.

"Will you do something for me?" I said, drying my face with her tissue. "Come with me to assembly? Help me get through this day? Not just the exam. There's something else I have to do. Don't make me go to the doctor yet. Please."

She kissed my forehead, took my hand in hers, and walked me over to the atrium.

CHAPTER
TWENTY-FOUR

When we got to the atrium, a sea of whispering girls sat in rows before the stage. Teachers sat in a line on chairs behind the podium, waiting for me.

"Ah, here she is!" the Head Teacher, Mr. Gillies, announced.

I made my way to the stage, clambered up the seemingly never-ending set of stairs, apologized to Mr. Gillies, took hold of the microphone, and stood at the podium. I tapped the microphone three times. "I'm so sorry I'm late," I said, and then began the pithy motivational speech I'd memorized:

"Girls of Aberfeldy Halls, it is my privilege to stand among you on the eve of our adult lives. The next few weeks will determine our success and our happiness. And we should ask ourselves: Are we proud? Have we done everything we can to achieve our goals?"

I faltered. My head was spinning. I felt as if I might faint. I couldn't remember the rest of my speech. And everything Amelia and I had agreed on went out of my head. We were supposed to go to the office after assembly—quietly, with discretion—but since talking to Mum, this seemed the wrong thing to do somehow. My whole body was shaking, throbbing, aching.

"And…there are other questions we need to ask ourselves…"

Oh good god, my breathing had turned into quick moans. Mum was approaching the stage, worried. Miss Rose was standing, moving closer, her arm out to catch me in case I should fall.

"Let me finish… There's one girl in particular, sitting among us, who should ask herself:

Are you scared?

Of getting caught…

Of losing control…

Being a failure…

Ruining everything?

Are you lonely?

Do you need help?"

Was I crying? Was Miss Rose taking hold of my arm and trying to get me to sit down?

I had to assert myself. I had to yell, "Who here wears size 8 underpants from Asda?"

Whispers turned to giggles.

"Does anyone here have a secret?" I pleaded, the giggles fading to silence as I pushed Miss Rose back towards her chair.

"Has something really scary happened that you don't want anyone to know about?"

"Mum, let me finish!" She was on stage now, her arm around my shoulder.

"Let me finish!" I snapped, flicking Mum's arm away. "Secrets are bad. We shouldn't keep them. We should never ask someone to keep them for us. It only makes things worse. From this moment on, there will be no more secrets. Please, please, please, think hard. Perhaps you don't even know. Perhaps your mind has gone all strange and you can't admit it happened. Can you come forward? Stand here in front of everyone and be unafraid? Just own up, here and now. Own up. In the words of Johann Friedrich von Schiller: 'It is wise to disclose what cannot be concealed.' No more secrets!"

I paused. The entire room was stunned, silent. The teachers were unsure what to do. As for me, black dots were buzzing before my eyes. Faces and chairs and walls were curvy and moving.

"Is it you, Viv?" I said, leaving the podium and walking to the very edge of the stage, trying to focus. "I saw the leaflet in your desk."

Viv Metstein turned bright red. Then bright white. "What leaflet?" she snarled.

"Amelia, stop them!" Mr. Gillies had yanked the microphone from my hand. My mother was trying to haul me from the stage.

Amelia didn't know what to do. She didn't expect me to make it all so public. She was gray-pale. She was shaking her head at me.

I turned to the chairs at the back of the stage. "Is it you, Miss Rose? I saw the note from *P*…"

Miss Rose fell into her chair and then slid as far down into it as possible, white as a ghost.

"Amelia, come up and help me!"

Amelia stood up. "Rachel, be quiet. This isn't the way. This isn't what we agreed. Remember? We're going to the office afterwards, after we've gotten something out of the fridge. You remember?"

Shit, the fridge. Mandy must be really cold. She'd be okay, I told myself. We'd wrapped her up nice and warm, and the vent was open.

Amelia's plea didn't deter me. "Is it you, the girl with the ponytail? Was it because of Mr. Burns?"

The girl with the ponytail ran out of the atrium.

Mr. Burns wriggled in his seat, shrugged at his fellow teachers and clasped his hands together so tightly they went green.

"Taahnya? Have you done it again? Did you leave it too late this time?"

Taahnya yelled angrily, "Shut her up, the retard!" She turned to Amelia, "Tell your best friend to shut up, the loony!"

Amelia looked really strange. She may even have been crying.

"Amelia?" I said, my eyes begging her to come forward.

Amelia put her head in her lap, sobbing.

"Amelia? Oh no, is it you after all? Amelia? That's why you're moving in with Piers…after all those times on the fire escape…It's not the eating dis…"

I was interrupted by the Head Teacher, who'd actually put his hand over my mouth to stop me talking.

After a struggle I freed my mouth and yelled.

"*Amelia O'Donohue. Confess! Tell us! Pleee…*"

Two hands were now over my mouth. And someone had switched the power off. The room went dark.

Amelia fled her mid-row chair. Several feet were stamped on. Several chairs were kicked over. Could it be her after all? Not bulimic. Not unaware. A mother. With psychiatric problems. An alien dropped down from a spaceship. A screwed up teenage mother in denial. Hiding from everyone, maybe even from herself, just as she'd said.

The teachers had now risen from their backstage chairs and

were trying to get the pupils out of the atrium. The girls were beginning to stand up.

"He's perfect!" I yelled, hoping Amelia would hear me and have the courage to come back. "He's a perfect, beautiful, captivating little boy. I've named him Sam. He's perfe…"

He's perfect, I thought, his gorgeous little face clear in my mind.

I didn't collapse gracefully, but it was slow. Slowly, down, down, to the spot at the front of the stage I'd been standing on, the place where a large pool of my own blood welcomed me. A pool of thick dark blood which splattered all over Mum and Miss Rose when it merged with the thump of my unconscious body.

CHAPTER
TWENTY-FIVE

Oh god, I hate hospitals. What kind of subconscious screw up means I want a job in a place I hate more than anything, except that island maybe? My mind's a mess. It's been a mess a while now. Do I really want to be a doctor? Why? To take control, to make sure I'm not the one who's lying in the bed waiting to be told the terrible news, but the one who's standing over the bed telling the terrible news? No doubt about it, my mind's a mess. Has been for a while now.

Do I really want to find out who had that baby?

I'm going there, aren't I? To the hospital. I'm on my way, lying on a stretcher inside some medical transport machine with uniformed medical types hovering over me with worried looks on their faces, probably saying to each other, "Ah, so this is Rachel Ross. The girl who'll spend the rest of her life in hospital…"

I don't want to go to hospital. I want to do my English exam. Everyone will be doing their English exam. I want to go back. I want to go back to the safe place, the hiding place I'd half put myself in since the age of nine, after I did that terrible thing. I want to go back to the even safer place I put myself in since arriving at Aberfeldy Halls, where nothing exists: not family, not island, not the good lord, not bullies, not ex-boyfriends, friends, ex-friends, nothing, not even my body or anything related to it, just nice safe work, work, and work.

Could I go back please? Could you please turn the ambulance around and take me back there?

"What's she saying?" one of the medical types hovering over me says to someone else. "Did you catch that?"

"It's all right, my darling Rachel," a third person says, and I realize the person isn't medical, she's my mum, and she's crying.

"Take me back," I say, but no one seems to hear me or understand me. My mask is in the way.

Always the mask. What is with the mask already? I want to take it off. I want to be maskless. Nebulizer free. I want to breathe on my own. I want to tell them, yell at them—do you not realize an actual person is at risk? Do you not realize a beautiful little boy is alone in a cupboard in a grotty, disused darkroom on the second floor of the dormitory building? Do you not realize that I have to go back now? We have to go back. Turn around now. *Do you not realize?!*

The key, I manage to say. *The key to the darkroom, it's in my blazer pocket. And Mandy, she's in the fridge.*

"Up the morphine," the faceless medical type says to someone I can't see.

And I fade.

Into darkness.

And through the darkness I see another Rachel.

She's at the island dance, nine months ago.

• • •

"Dance?" someone who makes me feel sick asks.

"Thought you chucked me." My past-voice wobbles and bounces in my head.

"Well, I'm picking you up again, aren't I?" he echoes. *Aren't I…Aren't I…*

He takes the Irn-Bru from my hand and puts it on the chair. "Come outside?"

And I know what it means to go outside. I know it means more than kissing. Am I ready yet? Am I ready to do more? If I'm not, I'm chucked. If I'm not, he'll go out with someone else. Because he's hot. He's cool. His parents are arty farty types. He's going to be an actor. If I don't, someone else will.

Even if his tongue's like sandpaper and he says the stupidest things like, "As they say in the fillems, this is very romantic." If I don't, he'll chuck me, for definite this time.

So I go. I don't want to be chucked. I don't want to stay at home while Mandy's down at the beach snogging Andrew, getting love-bites that require concealment in huge turtle-neck jumpers. I don't want to be any more miserable than I already am.

I go. And it's lucky we have nothing to say to each other because it's not necessary to talk. All I have to do is stand and hope the innards of my mouth will survive the tongue-massacre, then sit, then lie on the ground beside the wheelie bin and let myself let him.

It's far less pleasant than a conker up a nostril.

"Rachel Ross!" This voice comes from Mandy's mum—Mrs. Grogan. Usually I call her Aunty Jen. Usually she loves me. I'm her neighbor. I'm her daughter's best friend. My father lets her write stupid articles in the local newspaper about exceptionally straight carrots. He even pays her.

"Rachel Ross!" she yells, with a voice that indicates I should no longer call her Aunty. She has two large, full, black rubbish bags in her hands. She's about to put them in the wheelie bin, but now she's seen us.

"In here now!" she yells. And all I can think is *Oh no, Mrs. Grogan's seen John's bare bottom. It's good. It's firm. But I don't think she should see it. I don't think she'll like it.*

"Go to the toilet and stay there till I say," she snarls, once we're back inside the building. Already, everyone is stopping and looking.

"Please don't tell my mother and my father!" I say.

"It's not them you should worry about, Rachel Ross, it's the good lord."

"*him* again?" I say out loud. him with no capital h and big freaky underpants.

I feel guilty and ashamed and ill in the toilet. I sit on the plastic chipped seat and put my head in my hands and for a moment I wish I believed in the good lord because what I need now, more than anything, is to be saved. Please, someone, save me.

• • •

I open my eyes. I remember where I am. I just collapsed on the stage at assembly, in front of the whole school. I'm on a stretcher in an ambulance. And I can see them again, the medical types. They're whispering to each other. *How could this be? How could she not know?* And my mum shushes them and tells me to relax because I'm not in trouble and everything's going to be fine.

I decide I'm better off with my eyes closed, but then the moving pictures come back to the inside of my head, back from where I'd kept them hidden deep down inside somewhere, like letters in a shoebox in a cupboard, and they hurt my brain. But I can't stop them coming at me anyways. They're squeezing through the cracks, pushing, to get out.

• • •

It's nine months ago. I'm in the toilet at the island dance.

"Rachel? *Rachel!* Come with me now!" my mum says, and I open the toilet door.

She doesn't seem angry at me. She seems worried but not angry. She takes my hand, hauls me out of the bathroom, across the dance floor, and through the foyer. Everyone stops and stares. And here's a shock: while the crowd stare at me, all-knowing, snarling, giggling, judging, my mother yells:

"What the *f* are you looking at?" Not just f, you understand, but the whole caboodle, uck and all, and then she drags me outside and into our car, where Dad has the engine running.

My mother has just said the whole entire f word and I have just opened my eyes.

• • •

"You just said the f word," I say. I'm back in the present now. Mum's still sitting over me in the ambulance. My words aren't coming out right. I'm off my head. I'm pure off my head. This morphine has done my nut in. Mum can't understand what I'm saying. She's stroking my hair. She won't stop crying.

"Is he okay?" I try to say, but that drip is tremendous and stupendous, and I'm out of control. So this is what it feels like to be out of control. Even the word "okay" comes out fantastic. Something like *urghhhaaaa*: Sprawling, garbled, unleashed, free.

"She's delirious," someone says.

"No, I'm Rachel, and he's Sam," I say, concentrating on the shape my mouth should take to make the sounds work. I look at Mum and take my time with the next sentence. "Is...he... okay? Is...*Sam*...okay?"

"He's fine, my darling. Rest now. He's perfect. He's beautiful. We'll look after him."

I close my eyes and go backwards again.

• • •

To the kitchen table of our croft house. Nine months ago. "We have made a decision," my mother and my father—as I called them then—say. Looking at it from my half-dream, the house seems pretty. Suddenly I understand why tourists would want to come here for Hogmanay. "We're going to send you to Aberfeldy Halls."

I'm happy but I don't realize how lucky this is, because at Aberfeldy Halls I will need to hide even more than ever. There, I'll need to dig down so deep no one will find me. I'll need to cover myself with other peoples' secrets and when that becomes too much, I'll cover my ears with my hands and hum, not listening, not hearing, just studying, just thinking ahead to the job, the city, living alone in a place where no one will know me and no one will find me and no one will blame me.

• • •

Oh help me, I'm in the present again, in the ambulance. It's stopped quite suddenly. The brakes make my brain bounce against the back of my head and with the bounce, our pretty highland kitchen table flies from my mind. We've arrived at the hospital.

CHAPTER
TWENTY-SIX

I don't remember it for ages. Several people have to help me find the memory 'cause I've hidden it so well. Several people, mostly doctors, who arrive at the same time each day to talk to me. They use several methods, mostly talking ones, but they also give me medication.

After a few weeks, the methods begin to work, and I remember this:

I'm in my cubicle bed trying to sleep off the terrible pain I'm feeling, which I definitely don't want to feel. Not now. Not on the day before my first exam. I fall asleep and dream I'm late for my English exam, I'm falling out of the classroom window. I land. It hurts. Everyone looks down on me. I've screwed everything up, haven't I? I've ruined everything and everyone knows.

I realize now it wasn't landing on the ground that had hurt. It was him, arriving so suddenly, so painfully. It hurts so much I make noises farm animals make, then I shake so hard that reality spills right out of my head.

"Good, Rachel, Good," the doctors say.

Better as a dream, the insides of my mind apparently argued at the time. Better as a dream, my confused mind and body apparently argued in the hours afterwards.

"That's right, Rachel. Now we're getting somewhere."

• • •

And, bit by bit, I see the last nine months as they really were.

The first three: feeling ill all the time, craving cauliflower cheese and Sammy's chicken curries, thinking people smelled funny, taking people's secrets and hiding them inside me along with my own, blaming my parents and the island for all the scary strangeness.

The second three: blossoming, focused, working like a dog, cut off from Sammy and friends and family. Ignore them. Ignore everything. Work.

The third trimester: nesting, cleaning my cupboards, and smoothing my favorite red duvet over and over.

All the while a baby was growing inside me, pushing at me, yelling, "I'm here! I'm here!"

CHAPTER
TWENTY-SEVEN

Amelia O'Donohue here to see you," a nurse says, and I realize I want to see her more than anything. For weeks I've only seen my parents and people in coats or uniforms, all with notebooks and pens, questions, opinions, concerns, ways to help me.

"How you doing?" Amelia asks, putting some books and a tin of cupcakes with coconut-covered icing on my bedside table.

"I'm totally crazy, apparently."

She laughs, then holds my hand. "You caused quite a stir, Miss Rachel Ross."

"Don't tell me. I don't want to hear."

"I don't care if you don't want to hear. I'm going to tell you and you can tell whoever you want afterwards."

I smile. "Okay."

"The chef left his wife. He and Miss Rose have moved to Spain."

"No way."

Amelia was like, "Way. And Mr. Burns was sacked."

"Oh shit."

"No, don't worry, he deserved it. Three past pupils have come forward since."

"What about Mandy?"

"She fell asleep in the fridge, snug as a bug in the sleeping bag. She failed all but history. Starting hairdressing in Aberdeen. Apparently John chucked her 'cause she was a slut."

"See that guy…" I say, shaking my head.

"Is John involved at all?" she asks. "I mean, now?"

"His folks offered. We declined…How's Louisa?"

"English at Oxford."

"Oh…good, I'm pleased for her."

"I hated your guts for a while, telling everyone about my eating like that."

"I'm so sorry, Amelia." And I really am.

"It's okay," she says. "It was the best thing that could have happened, Dr. Halliday says. All out in the open now, and I have to deal with it. So I've decided not to move in with Piers, not till I've sorted it out. "

"Good plan," I say.

Amelia looks through a pile of books she's brought for me and takes one out that looks nothing like a novel. After a moment, I recognize it—it's the diary I stole from her.

"Seeing as you're so interested..." she says with a wry smile. "I'll continue where you left off."

"How did you know?" I bite my lower lip with shame, but Amelia's high chin and smug smile tell me all's okay.

"You put it back on the wrong side of the desk."

Blimey, I never knew she was so particular.

"OMG like where do I start?" she reads. "That kid in the cupboard? It was only Rachel Ross's! Like my only friend here. And I had no idea. And neither did she! What the fudge! Next we'll not know if we're girls or boys or alive or dead or vampires or bloody hamsters. And today Rachel only like exposed the whole entire school for the screwed up turds they are. Most excellent! And I thought a bit of puking was an issue! GASP! And guess what? Ten minutes ago this boy Rachel liked just knocked on my cubicle door. Don't know how he got in the building. I nearly died. He's really cute. And I think he's like in love with her or something. Anyways, I told this boy Sammy all about it and he cried. He even asked if he could see the baby, but Rachel's father had taken him to the hospital with the social worker. I've never seen a boy cry before. I was like, 'Stop crying, you retard.' And he was like: 'But is that it for us then? Is that it? Does that mean it's really never going to happen? My dad'll be so upset. He agreed with me. He thought she was the one.' I had to call Miss Rose to take him away in the end. She was very nice to him. Didn't get him into trouble at all. Now I am pure buzzing. Today was the most exciting day I've ever had. Ah…F*** it all…I'm starving. I've got macaroons but apparently they have potatoes in them. Gross!"

Amelia stops reading because I'm snort-laughing and I can't stop. I end up writhing on the floor with an ache in my middle that I would've described as the worse stomach pain ever before some daft idiot retrieved my memory of labor. (Could they not have let that one stay where it was?)

Near-peeing done, I get back into my bed, exhausted, and Amelia reads from her favorite childhood book. It's about fairies. Her words twinkle on me. I fall asleep.

CHAPTER
TWENTY-EIGHT

A few months after getting out of hospital, I meet Sammy for a coffee. He seems a bit nervous when I approach his table, so I sit down and make it as easy for him as I can.

"I didn't think you'd come," I say. "I'm, well, complicated. I thought you'd run a mile."

"I still might," he answers. There's an awkward pause.

"Three surprising things," I say. "When I was nine, I told my dad my mum was having an affair. When I was sixteen, I lost my virginity to a boy I didn't even like beside a wheelie bin. And I have never successfully used a tampon."

He smiles at me. But he's still a bit uncertain. I don't blame him.

"Oh, and remember how you told me about the three essential ingredients for happiness?"

"Fresh air, exercise, and giggling…" he says.

"Yeah. Well, I've worked out the fourth ingredient…"

"You have?"

"I have." Slowly, I lean over the table, moving my face towards his. He doesn't move an inch, but he doesn't have to. When I kiss him—a soft, long, closed-mouth kiss—he takes a while to respond. When he does, it's worth the wait.

I move my head away from his and sit in my chair, proud that I had worked out that the most important ingredient to happiness is *giving*.

"Actually, I was thinking curry," he says, breaking into a smile. And then a laugh. The ice is broken.

"I want to tell you all about this new recipe I've created," he says, plonking a large brown paper bag on the table before me. "It's called Sammy's Lamb Sensation. It's so good it puts you in a trance-like state."

"You know, I think I'm just about ready to eat lamb again," I say.

I don't know what's going to happen. But he's not going to run a mile.

CHAPTER
TWENTY-NINE

When I get home—ten containers of Sammy's curry in hand—a report has arrived on the doorstep.

REPORT TO THE CHILDREN'S PANEL

NAME: SAM ROSS

ADDRESS: 2/2, 178 ARGYLL STREET, GLASGOW

Sam Ross was born in the dormitory of Aberfeldy Halls, a girls' boarding school in Perthshire, Scotland. His mother, seventeen-year-old Rachel Ross, abandoned him in a linen cupboard shortly after giving birth.

The attached psychiatric report indicates that the mother had been suffering from a condition known as denied pregnancy, where the mother hides the fact that she is pregnant. As argued in this report:

Women who deny pregnancy are usually the good girls in a very difficult, either chaotic or dysfunctional, family. They are the cheerleaders, they are the leaders. They are also very isolated. The will to conceal the pregnancy is so strong in these women that not only do they hide it from the people closest to them, unconsciously they conceal it from themselves. They can even suppress their physical symptoms. By not telling anyone, the pregnancy remains unreal.

In the case of Rachel Ross, she did conceal the pregnancy from herself. She ignored any symptoms and gained little weight, her bump barely visible within the cavities of her petite pear-shaped frame. Rachel Ross states that she continued to have her period throughout the pregnancy and was not aware in any way of the massive changes her body was undergoing.

While the subject must have been conscious of her labor and of giving birth, she appears to have undergone some kind of psychotic episode following delivery (see attached report). After having the baby in the bed of her tiny cubicle, she clamped and cut the cord, hid the child in the linen cupboard, changed her sheets, showered, and fell asleep. When she woke, she had no recollection of the birth and became confused and disorientated, embarking on what she calls a "who had it"—an investigation to find out who had given birth. Her good friend, Amelia O'Donohue, assisted her in this endeavor. During this twelve-hour investigation, Rachel Ross cared for the child in the darkroom of the school, unintentionally bonding with her baby in the process.

As outlined in the psychiatric report, the mother seems to have been under a significant amount of stress at school. At the time, she felt unsupported by her parents and desperate to succeed at school in order to flee them and the island-home she hated. She had also suffered some degree of bullying by her old friends. The combination of these pressures may have resulted in the denial of her pregnancy.

Medical reports indicate that no harm came to the child as a result of the mother's actions. In fact, he appears to be thriving and at the time of writing is a healthy 10 pounds 8 ounces.

After Rachel Ross collapsed at school, she was taken to Perth Hospital. She had lost a lot of blood, and the stress had possibly sparked a serious asthma attack. She was treated successfully and allowed to return to the family home after three weeks. She is now healthy and living at home with her parents, at 2/2 178 Argyll Street, Glasgow.

Rachel Ross now appears to have a supportive and loving relationship with her parents. Archie and Claire Ross have made it clear that they will help their daughter bring up the child—indeed, they seem besotted with him. According to the parents, they had always wanted a second child, but work pressures, marital problems, and an early menopause had conspired against them.

Despite being unable to sit her exams, Rachel Ross was allowed to do her exams several weeks after the birth. She gained the second highest marks in the school. She says she is proud to have come second to her old friend Louisa MacDonald.

Rachel has just started her medical degree at the University of Glasgow. Her parents are delighted to finance her studies and to take care of baby Sam while she is there.

In the writer's opinion, there is no need for compulsory measures of care for baby Sam. He is well loved and well looked after. As a result, the writer recommends that no further action be taken in this case.

I finish the report and walk over to the window, where Mum and Dad are huddled over the crib, arm in arm. I force myself between them for a gentle family cuddle, no elbows. Sam gurgles happily, a soft breeze washing over him from Kelvinside Park.

I inhale the breeze and soak in the view: the art galleries, the university, the people walking, the buses honking.

Sam starts crying. The honk has scared him.

"My turn to hold him. I'll give you £5 each," says Mum.

"No mine," says Dad. "Or I'll pour freezing water over your heads."

And even though I have a lecture in ten minutes, I'm like, "Out of my way, you old fogies, he's mine."

ACKNOWLEDGMENTS

Thanks to Daniel Ehrenhaft; to everyone at Sourcebooks Fire; to my agents, Allan Guthrie and Lucy Juckes at Jenny Brown Associates; to Ciorstan Campbell, Karen Campbell, Evie McGowan, Alex Kelloway, and Anna Casci, for their thoughts and advice; and a big thanks to Blether Media for the fab book trailer.

ABOUT THE AUTHOR

One of thirteen children, Helen FitzGerald left her native Australia to get some attention. She worked as a parole officer and prison social worker in Glasgow for more than ten years. Her gritty and steamy adult thrillers have been translated into numerous languages and widely praised as glorious black comedy. *Amelia O'Donohue Is So Not a Virgin* is her first novel for young adults. Helen is married to screenwriter Sergio Casci and has two children. Visit her website www.helenfitzgerald.co.uk.